KU-722-732

Loveless Love

Loveless Love

Luigi Pirandello

Translated by J.G. Nichols

ET REMOTISSIMA PROPE

Modern Voices

Modern Voices
Published by Hesperus Press Limited
4 Rickett Street, London SW6 1RU
www.hesperuspress.com

Published thanks to financial support from the Italian Ministry of
Foreign Affairs

Originally published in Italian as *Amori senza amore* in 1894
Copyright: © 1995, Arnoldo Mondadori Editore Spa, Milano
This translation first published by Hesperus Press Limited, 2002
Reprinted and reset, 2005
Introduction and English language translation © J.G. Nichols, 2002

Designed and typeset by Fraser Muggeridge studio
Printed in Jordan by the Jordan National Press

ISBN: 1-84391-410-7

All rights reserved. This book is sold subject to the condition that it shall not be
resold, lent, hired out or otherwise circulated without the express prior consent
of the publisher.

Contents

Introduction

Luigi Pirandello (1867–1936) was more or less contemporary with Sigmund Freud (1856–1939). We may at times have to remind ourselves of their nineteenth-century origin, since in this, the next century but one, it can often seem that they are more at grips with our current concerns than many of our contemporaries are. And they have much in common. This is not to suggest any influence of either one on the other, but simply to note that they are involved in a way of thinking which dominated intellectual life in their time and has remained a preoccupation in ours. They are concerned with revealing the motives of human conduct, and not only the motives which we hide from others, but also those which remain hidden from ourselves.

There are differences, of course. Freud, a psychiatrist, was engaged, while attempting to heal his patients, in formulating theories which would, he hoped, clarify some of the hidden workings of the human mind: theories which, once formulated, could be applied universally. Though interested in myth and literature, and happy to use mythological and literary characters and incidents, as he used his patients, to illustrate his theories, he was primarily a scientist. Pirandello, on the other hand, was an artist, and so with him theory is less significant than the presentation of concrete situations and people. In these first stories of his at least, he does not theorise at all: he simply shows. He records what happens and what is said (always in Pirandello a very important part of what happens), and leads us to what seem to be inevitable conclusions which need no abstract formulation.

The works of both men can still at times make us feel uncomfortable, as though we would perhaps rather not be told, or anyway rather not believe, what they are telling us. In one very important respect Pirandello is more disturbing than Freud. Freud's theories were based on his dealings with people who were mentally disturbed, and so we can always tell ourselves that his findings, even if true, may very well not apply to those who are not mental patients. With Pirandello this escape is not available: his characters tend to be, and in this early work all certainly are, people whom we must call normal, whatever that may be. They may be absurd and ill-advised, but they are also ordinary people in ordinary situations, and their absurdity and foolishness are very close to home.

Since *Loveless Love* was the first volume of short stories which Pirandello published, there can be a temptation to look in these stories for some foreshadowing of the writer which he was to become. Certainly no one who reads them in this way will be disappointed. For instance, much of the narrative is conveyed by dialogue, and this looks forward to the plays, now usually considered to be Pirandello's greatest achievement: when he was awarded the Nobel Prize for Literature in 1934 it was explicitly stated that it was for his dramatic work. (The second story in this book was indeed, very many years later, rewritten as a play.) And above all, the disjunction in human life between what *is* and what *seems*, with its attendant difficulty of deciding what is reality, is already his theme.

What is love? Pirandello does not explicitly ask this question in these three stories, but he does answer it, and in several different ways, none of which makes love sound very loving. A landlord enjoys falling in love with his tenants. He has in fact made a study of it, and has developed a procedure for expressing it, with another procedure for getting himself off the hook when he tires of it. He can be said to be a very loving person, only if by that we mean someone who loves many people. But then he has a tenant for whom his feelings are different, and rather disconcerting, since they are increased by her indifference. Indeed, that indifference is really what he at first falls in love with. Then, when she is jilted, he falls in love with her misfortune. Finally he is in love with what he regards as his triumph over his former rival. In the second story a woman is loved by a man whom she does not like, and who is not sufficiently enamoured to bring himself to declare his love without being pushed. The man whom she does apparently love, returns her love, but he continues to love himself rather more. Ultimately she decides to marry someone whom she scarcely knows, and whose reputation is dubious, apparently because he is the only one who has not yet had the opportunity to reveal his shortcomings. In the third story a woman attracts advances which she then repels, so her would-be suitors find wives elsewhere. She is a very accomplished and capable woman, and helps the new husbands and wives in every way she can, with the result that the husbands fall in love with the unattainable ideal she represents. She is herself in love with – what? With power? With the desire for revenge? With being loved?

That nothing turns out as people expect does not mean that they are shown as the playthings of fate. It is rather that they are driven by someone, or something, which is inside themselves but remains hidden from them. The accomplished flatterer, whose pleasure lies in remaining uncommitted while he controls the feelings of others, ends up not in control of the situation but under the control of his own feelings. Or again, a male protagonist's subtle and unscrupulous scheming is decisive in persuading a woman to marry the very man whom he deplores. The ancient temple of Apollo at Delphi was inscribed with the precept, often cited as the beginning of wisdom, 'Know thyself'. A suitable epigraph to these three stories might well be, 'Thou canst not know thyself'. The characters in them think they know themselves and understand their own motives, and at first we think that we do too, but they, to some extent, and we completely are gradually shown better.

These are bleak narratives of mistakes and frustrations. Why then are they so enjoyable? The answer is, I think, that, even if we cannot know ourselves, we are still creatures with an irresistible urge to know, and we even enjoy getting to know that we cannot know. Pirandello's birthplace was Cavusù, which in Sicilian means 'chaos'. It is a kind of chaos of which he writes, but his way of doing so is both controlled and calm. We can enjoy in art what we would find unbearable in life.

– J.G. Nichols, 2002

Note on the Text:
The translation is based on the Italian text: Luigi Pirandello, *Amori senza amore*, Edizioni Studio Tesi, 1994.

Loveless Love

The Wave

I

Giulio Accurzi was what is known in society as a fine young man: thirty-three, well-to-do, smartly dressed, not unintelligent. He had moreover, in the opinion of his friends, one speciality: he was always falling in love with his tenants.

His house had two floors. He let the lower floor, which included a terrace overlooking a pleasant little garden. This garden could only be entered by means of a narrow staircase which ran from inside the upper floor, where he lived with his paralysed mother who had been confined to a chair for some years.

From time to time his friends failed to see anything of him, and then they could be quite certain that Giulio Accurzi had started making himself amiable to the *filia hospitalis* on the floor below.

For him these flirtations were one of the comforts of his property. The tenant, the father, was gratified to note the charming manners and the delicate attentions of the owner of the house, while the daughter could never tell for sure whether these attentions were really a consequence of the charming manners, as her father argued, or of love, as at times it seemed she had been led to believe.

Giulio Accurzi showed considerable talent in this.

During the first months of the lease he would flirt from his balcony down onto the terrace. That was the first stage, known as *loving below*. Then he went on to the second stage. This was *loving above*, that is from the garden to the terrace, and it normally happened at the start of spring. This was when he would send the old gardener again and again to the lower floor with presents of bunches of flowers – violets, geraniums, lilies... Sometimes he went so far as to allow himself to cast up from the garden, with the utmost courtesy, some magnificent *alba plena* into the two rosy hands held out in expectation above. And the moon was a witness from on high to these scenes, as Giulio Accurzi playfully bent down to caress the girl's shadow which was projected from the terrace onto the golden sand of the garden. The girl, from the marble balustrade, would laugh softly and shake her head, or else she would suddenly draw back so that her shadow might elude the innocent caress. But that was as far as it must go. And if it went any further there was a ready way out. He would tell the father that he was sorry, but 'with the new year he had to raise the rent'. His contracts with his tenants were always for one year.

Before his mother had become so gravely ill, Giulio Accurzi had never thought seriously about taking a wife.

'And yet you would be an ideal husband!' his friends used to say to him. 'You are someone who likes ease and comfort in love. Just turn your two floors into one floor!'

2

When Signora Sarni came with her daughter to live on the lower floor, Agata had been engaged for three years to Mario Corvaja, who was at that time in Germany completing his studies in philology. The engagement had had its ups and downs, and it seemed as though the date for the wedding was being obscured once more by clouds of uncertainty. It was true that Mario Corvaja would soon be returning from Germany, but who knows how long he would have to wait for a vacancy for a chair of philology in the university.

Giulio Accurzi knew nothing of all this, and so he could think of no reason for Signorina Sarni's mournful countenance. It was only rarely that he saw her on the terrace, in the evening, wan, with a pale rose-pink shawl over her shoulders, and a black dress.

From the balcony he observed every little act of hers. She liked to stop and look at two canaries in a cage hanging from a pole on the terrace – two little creatures that sang happily all the day; or she would pause to study the vases of flowers lined up on the marble balustrade, of which her mother, Donna Amalia Sarni, took extraordinary care. The girl gathered two or three violets, then she withdrew, as though possessed by other thoughts, without casting a glance at the garden below, or raising her eyes, even momentarily, to the balcony, where Giulio Accurzi, coughing slightly from time to time, or deliberately moving his chair about, was consumed with rage and irritation at her indifference.

These poor violets, sealed up in a letter, and squashed from being stamped so many times in the post, had to cover much ground, and go far, far away, as far as Heidelberg on the Rhine, up there in the north... What did Giulio Accurzi know about that?

He was enchanted by the gentle air of peace which reigned on the lower floor of that house, full of fresh flowers and light, an almost conventual peace and silence. Donna Amalia, tall and grand, with a face that was calm and still beautiful despite her sixty years, with a steady tread, and never discomposed, looked after the affairs of the house; then, towards evening, she attended to the flowers, just as in the morning she had attended to her religious duties, for she was very devout.

The daughter led a different life. She got up late, played the piano for a while, more as a distraction than as a pleasure; then, after breakfast, she would read or embroider; in the evening, she either went out for a while with her mother, or stayed at home and read or played the piano: she never went to church or dealt with household matters, ever. Nevertheless there was between the mother and the daughter perfect harmony, a silent understanding, always.

Every now and then the silence of the house was broken by the arrival of Signora Amalia's other daughter, married to Cesare Corvaja, Mario's brother. She always brought along her two toddlers, and their auntie was delighted to see them.

Only then, without knowing why, did Giulio Accurzi, shut up all day in the house, feel his heart fill with joy: from his balcony he saw the children and Signorina Sarni burst out onto the terrace, he sensed their smiles, and he heard the tender sound of her voice; he saw her bend down towards her nephew and niece, who coaxed her, flinging their arms around her neck; and as he watched all this he smiled happily, blissfully.

'Where's daddy, Rorò?'

'A long way away... A long way away...' replied Rorò, closing his eyes and dragging the words out, with his little face thrust forward.

Cesare Corvaja was the first engineer on steamers belonging to the General Italian Shipping Company, and he went on voyages to America.

'What will daddy bring you, Mimì, when he comes back?'

'Lots of things...' replied Mimì placidly.

Meanwhile, inside the house, the mother and her elder daughter were talking about Agata, about how she had changed after the promise of marriage, and particularly after the deadly illness from which she had only with difficulty recovered, thanks to the care she had received from Mario Corvaja's parents.

'Obstinate!' sighed her mother. 'She won't listen to reason. She doesn't want to understand... And yet she realises that he doesn't love her any more! Some nights I can hear her weeping quietly... It's breaking my heart, believe me; but I don't know what to say to her. I'm always afraid that horrible illness will return...'

'What madness! What a tragedy!' exclaimed the sister for her part: she had been against the idea of the marriage right from the beginning.

What could Giulio Accurzi know of all this, intent as he was on enjoying from his balcony the caresses Agata gave to the children and the children's coaxing of their auntie?

3

Towards the end of summer Agata fell seriously ill. The slightest thing tired her out. Her hidden suffering, her hidden melancholy, had gradually transformed itself into boredom. She stayed in bed longer, awake, with a vacant mind; she had completely lost her appetite, and no longer listened to any of the words of encouragement or comfort, or any of the complaints of her mother and sister.

Giulio Accurzi, alarmed one day by the grave news brought to him by his old gardener, went so far as to question the doctor on his way out. The latter's reply disturbed him in two ways: he gathered on that occasion only that Signorina Sarni was engaged to be married, and that her fiancé was expected to arrive within days now that her illness had taken such a bad turn.

'Ah! So she's engaged!'

From that day he was no longer at peace. He made every effort to convince himself that it was really foolish to take so much interest 'in the health of one of his tenants'. He forced himself to go out; but it took him two hours to get dressed, because every now and then he had to go onto the balcony to see if anyone had appeared on the terrace below. Why? He did not himself know why! Certainly not to ask after her: that would not have seemed to him the right thing to do. Perhaps in order to discover the seriousness of the illness from the expression on someone's face. And every time, to put an end to his expectations, which even he saw were childish, he took refuge in another childish action: he started to count to a hundred.

'If in the meantime no one appears, I will go away.'

And he began slowly:

'One... two... three...'

Then, as he counted, his mind would wander and only his lips went on murmuring the numbers. Sometimes, with his hat on his head, ready to go out, he managed to count to thirty; in the end he got tired, and slipped through the door. He had to force himself not to pause to eavesdrop on the ground-floor landing. Once outside, he avoided his friends, and could not distract himself. He walked round a little, without any object, and was very bored. And, at the end, as though struck by a sudden thought, he hurriedly retraced his steps.

'Perhaps by now he will have arrived!'

He waited anxiously for Agata's fiancé. He was consumed by the longing to see him, to make his acquaintance, without really knowing the reason for his curiosity.

His mother, although by now she no longer took any interest in anything, being tired of everything, even of waiting and calling for death, had become aware of the change that had come over her son; and one morning she said:

'Giulio, don't act like an idiot!'

'What do you mean – an idiot, Mama?' replied Giulio Accurzi, in whom by now his mother's way of speaking, the tone of her voice, and the movement of her head, inspired more irritation than sympathy.

And yet he had perhaps done something silly. Yes, he realised that himself and was disturbed by it. He had stopped Agata's sister, Erminia, on the staircase, and from the way in which he had spoken to her he was afraid that she might have suspected that he was so foolish as to entertain ideas in relation to her sister, although she was engaged to another.

'Who knows what she may have thought of me! Stupid...'

Deep down he did not want to admit to himself that he had fallen in love with Signorina Sarni.

'There has never been anything between her and me...'

And then he did his best to think of Agata as of anyone for whom he might feel some sympathy, knowing that her health was in a bad state.

'Poor young woman!' he said to himself. 'Such a nice person!... And that imbecile who doesn't come back! If he delays much longer, he will not see her...'

4

The comings and goings on the stairs became more and more frequent. From the upper landing Giulio, leaning over the banisters, observed who came and went. Other doctors had rushed to the sickbed, and two Sisters of Charity, and then a tall old man with a long white beard, Don Giacomo Corvaja, who had come in from the country expressly. Giulio gathered that the acute stage of the illness had passed, but that nevertheless the sick woman, overcome by extreme weakness, was subject to hysterical frenzies which drove her almost mad...

'They've cut off her hair and spoilt it!... You can hardly recognise her any more...' the serving maid had told him. 'She keeps asking for her fiancé... It looks as though he doesn't want to come back any more... If you only saw how things are down below...'

'He doesn't want to come back any more? What? He would leave her to die like this?' wondered Giulio, eating his heart out.

From time to time the door on the floor below opened noisily, and someone went out, rushing down the stairs. Then Giulio would rouse suddenly from his daydreams and grow pale...

'What can have happened?... Is she dying?...'

Then there are other people on the landing down there – Donna Amalia, Erminia, with drawn faces... Who are they expecting? A carriage has stopped in front of the main entrance. Look, it's him, Mario Corvaja, the fiancé! He is with the tall old man with the long white beard, his father. At long last he has come back!

'Well, how is she?' asks Mario anxiously of her mother. He is pale, and his brows are knitted. Then they all go back in, and the door is shut again.

Now where had Giulio heard that voice before? Yes, he knew Mario Corvaja by sight. Was he then Agata's fiancé? And what was going on down there, at that moment, in the sick woman's bedroom? Giulio tried hard to imagine the scene of their meeting. After an hour or so he saw Mario Corvaja leaving with his father. Giulio's eyes followed him from the balcony along the sunlit road. Where was he taking himself off to? Why was he gesticulating so animatedly as he spoke to his father? And he had left the sick woman so soon? In what sort of state was she?

Towards evening Giulio saw Don Giacomo Corvaja returning without his son. He learned later that Mario had set off again for Rome on the very day of his arrival. And so his return had been like a phantasmal apparition. The next day Agata left for the country with her mother and Don Giacomo Corvaja.

Giulio Accurzi guessed that the marriage plans of Mario

Corvaja and Agata Sarni had come to nothing. What had happened? She had fallen sick because of him, and he had abandoned her! But why? What more could the idiot want? How could he fail to love a creature who to him, Giulio Accurzi, seemed so worthy of love? And she perhaps was lamenting his loss.

As these thoughts ran through his head, he felt a sort of jealousy, a muffled regret, almost rancour... Could he himself do nothing about this? It was almost as though he would have liked to intervene in the matter – he felt so irritated by the actions of that idiot... Intervene! But how?

'And they have carried her off to his country house! Idiots! And why should they do that? How can they get her mind off it over there?' So he thought in the midst of his agitation. 'It would be much better if she were to die there...'

5

It so happened however, about a month later, that he found himself descending the stairs when the carriage, on its return from the Corvajas' place in the country, stopped in front of the main entrance of his house. Giulio Accurzi could not refrain from starting and exclaiming his surprise at the sight of Agata, who was getting out of the carriage, supported by her mother. Upset, and with his hands trembling, he ran to give some help to the two ladies; he offered his arm to the convalescent, and he supported her up the difficult climb, repeating at every step: 'Gently...like this... Lean on me, Signorina! Gently!'

At the door she thanked him shyly, with her eyes cast down, and lowering her head. In his confusion he reddened and, as soon as the door had closed, murmured:

'How weak she is!'

And immediately after:

'How she loved him!'

He forgot that he had been about to go out, and went on slowly climbing the steps, slapping his legs with the gloves which he held in his hand.

'How weak she is!' he repeated under his breath, pausing indecisively at the door of the house. Automatically he took the key out of his pocket and went in.

Then he heard his mother calling him, and he immediately ran to her, surprised to find himself in his own house.

'What have you forgotten?' his mother asked him in her nasal voice, wearily, with her head leaning to one side, swathed as always in a black woollen headscarf.

'No... nothing... I got bored... You know what? Our tenants from the floor below have come back...'

'I see!' sighed his mother wearily, bending her head to the other side, and she closed her eyes.

That exclamation and that movement irritated Giulio.

'The young lady has been very poorly, and she is still sick,' he said hurriedly, in a resentful tone of voice.

'She's young, never fear, she'll get better!' responded the invalid in the same voice as before and without opening her eyes.

Giulio went back into his room and sat down in an armchair, without thinking of taking off his hat or putting down his gloves and stick.

'How she loved him!' he murmured once more to himself, shaking his head slowly for a long while, with staring eyes. 'And that imbecile...'

He rose from the chair and walked up and down the room with his head bent...

He had seen her again; he had offered her his arm, he had felt the pleasant weight of that passion-worn body, and he would have liked to carry her in his arms to spare her the bother of that ascent... In her pallor and weariness she had seemed to him even more beautiful!

And she had thanked him...

6

For Giulio Accurzi there followed two weeks of continual agitation. Agata was no more to be seen on the terrace, and she never went out of the house. To his repeated question: 'How is the young lady?' the only answer he got from the servants was, 'Better,' followed by, 'She is well now,' and nothing more. He did not wish to appear indiscreet. Meanwhile he was not working any longer. As a matter of fact he had always worked very little. But previously, at least, he liked to study and to read, and so he had become a man of wide and various culture. Now he did not succeed in getting to the bottom of a page, even if it was a novel he was reading. Instead, he took much more care of his appearance: in front of the mirror he was distressed by his blond hair which was gradually thinning, especially on the left side, raising his brow a little too much; he became meticulous over everything relating to his hairstyle: he wanted to be impeccable. But then, after so much study and so much care, he did not go out of the house, but sat or leant on the iron railings of the balcony, and waited... Towards evening he saw Donna Amalia Sarni come out onto the terrace to water the flowers, and he followed attentively the rose of the watering can as it shed minute drops onto every vase, and he lingered over every vase as long as the watering can did. In this way he made the circuit of the balustrade. Some days he lost heart living such a pointless kind of life. He would have liked to go on a journey. But then! To whom could he entrust his mother?

One day, quite unexpectedly, he saw Erminia Corvaja's two

children burst out noisily onto the terrace, as they used to do, followed by their auntie. At that sound, even before she appeared on the terrace, Giulio Accurzi's heart began to throb violently. At long last he was seeing her! She seemed to him a different person... She was laughing!

'It's her... it's her... it's her...' he repeated to himself, trembling, as he drew back from the balcony. He returned immediately, but she had already left the terrace, taking the children with her.

He could no longer remain alone in his room: he felt the need to communicate his joy to someone. He took himself off to his mother, without knowing precisely what he would say to her. He found her in her usual position: with her head bent to one side and her eyes shut; she looked dead! The shutters of the two windows were slightly open, and the room was in a gloomy half-light.

'Are you asleep, Mama?' he asked softly, leaning over her, and lifting his mother's cold, waxen hand from where it lay on the arm of the chair.

'No, my son,' she sighed as she lay there without opening her eyes.

At the sound of that voice Giulio's mood immediately altered. It seemed to him then that he had never before realised what a disaster had befallen his mother. In a flash he saw her once more, still brisk, on her feet, always dressed in black after the death of his father, attending to her household affairs; there flashed in front of his eyes the vague sight of his mother, quite different from how she was in all his other memories, standing in evening dress in front of a large wall-mirror... one evening long ago. There was a man fastening a fine necklace about her neck: that was Giulio Accurzi's father; he was himself a very young child at that time; and this was the one, indistinct memory which he had of his father. Immediately afterwards he saw his mother once more, as she fell across the table, suddenly stricken by paralysis, while the two of them were having a meal. He looked at her, touched to the quick: it was now six years since she had been like this, forgotten by death, abandoned by life.

'Poor Mama!' he sighed, raising her cold, unfeeling hand to his lips; and the sound of her voice brought tears to his eyes.

'What do you want to tell me?' asked the invalid, without moving her head, as though she expected her son to make some confession.

'Mama…'

'Shush, shush, I know… Marry her, my son, if she is a good girl. Marry her, it would please me…'

And she turned her head away, sighing.

'What are you saying, Mama?'

'I'm saying marry her! It is time that you did… It would please me.'

'But do you know who she is, Mama?'

'Yes, I know it all.'

'I love her…' said Giulio, and he was immediately struck by the fact that he had used that word even to himself.

'Make yourself happy!' said his mother in conclusion.

He was perplexed. So his mother thought that Agata loved him in return? And on the contrary… And he had once more that uncertain feeling of rancour.

The invalid added:

'You will introduce us?'

'Of course…' replied Giulio uneasily; he said goodbye to his mother and left the room, sighing bitterly.

Why was he now overcome by sadness? Had not his mother always been like that, since she was taken ill? Yes, yes… but now…

He could not really define the cause of that sadness; but

nothing in the world would ever comfort him if he could not ultimately emerge from his state of indecision.

7

As soon as she set foot in her own home, Agata felt how pointless and hard her life would be henceforth. Her mother had immediately started to busy herself with the house, which had been left untouched for so long.

Agata went through the rooms, and she felt that she could find nowhere to sit in any of them, even for a moment, and nothing to do in the days following, in the long and tedious days which the future had in store for her. While still standing, she managed to strike one note on the piano, as if in order to hear the sound of the instrument again, and she went away immediately, as if she had been attacked. Oh, if only she had been able to follow her mother through those rooms, utterly intent on tidying everything up, and dusting the furniture!

She would have liked everyone to believe that she was not thinking of Mario Corvaja any longer, and above all that she was not in the least upset by the abandonment of her marriage. But how could she devote herself, in that crushing boredom, to the pain and effort of that pretence?

However, the recollection was too vivid and intense, and she not only had much to recall, but also much to regret from those four years of vain expectation. And she still did not really know the way he had avoided her when she was ill! She still kept all his letters in a little box, and now, shut up in her room, she reread them one by one. She sat down on the floor with a lighted candle, and consigned the letters to its flames, one after another, once she had reread them.

They were all ordered according to their dates, and bound in years, in four bundles. The largest bundle was the first, and the last one was very slight. After she had read them, she remained with her swollen eyes fixed upon the quivering flame: her mind went back over the day of the letter's date, while with trembling hand she brought the page up to the candle; then she sighed, and waited until the paper was completely reduced to ashes.

Giulio Accurzi meanwhile, after a night for reflection, full of doubts and hesitations, had resolved to go to see her sister, to whom he had on one occasion spoken and possibly revealed his feelings.

'There is no doubt,' he was thinking, 'that her relatives will be glad to accede to my request. But she herself, Agata? She has never taken any notice of me; she doesn't even know that I am alive… At this moment she is thinking of "someone completely different".'

He was well aware that to be reasonable he should have let a little more time pass before making his request; but jealousy and *amour-propre* would not allow him to do this. He would know no peace as long as the memory of the other man remained in Agata's heart, and on the other hand he wished to feign complete ignorance of the fact that she had been promised to Mario Corvaja. Giulio Accurzi felt that if she refused him he would immediately begin to hate her in every way in which hate may reveal itself. One thought more than any other discouraged him: 'Perhaps one day he will see me with her, in love with her, and he will look at me with eyes full of commiseration… "Yes, that lady loved me, and I did not want her… I *abandoned* her. Now she has found a ninny to fall for her. And there he is over there…"'

Erminia Corvaja was very surprised by Giulio Accurzi's visit. Pale and nervous, he began by getting lost in superficial commonplaces, then all at once, on an impulse, he came out with:

'Signora, just hear the reason for my visit…' But suddenly he stopped. 'I should like her to give me…'

He was about to say: 'Some explanation.' He reddened in his confusion; and then he began again: 'Look, you know that your mother lives in my house. I have been fortunate enough to appreciate the truly rare qualities of the Signora as much as those of the Signorina your sister… I hope that she is now well… I saw her yesterday, I think it was, when you came with the children… Yes… it was yesterday… It seemed to me that…'

'Oh, yes, now… her health at least is better…' concluded Erminia Corvaja uncomfortably, trying to smile. And she lowered her eyes.

Giulio Accurzi took note of that *at least*, and he wriggled about in his armchair, not finding any way now in which he could reopen the discussion.

'Yes… I knew… that she had been ill… I did in fact ask after her on one occasion… you remember? Yes… But now fortunately that is past… I happened to be present when she returned from your father-in-law's home, didn't I? Yes… The poor young lady!… She was suffering so much…'

'Yes, it's true that she has suffered a great deal,' agreed Erminia Corvaja, shaking her head.

Again Giulio Accurzi wriggled about in his armchair.

'Now that is past, however…' he repeated. 'And when an illness can be talked about… It was a pity I could not come down on that occasion… but my mother, poor thing… Perhaps you know that…'

'Oh, yes, such a pity… I know, poor lady!…' said Erminia, with an air of deep commiseration.

'It's been six years!…' Giulio exclaimed. And having taken that turn, the conversation continued more easily for a while. He did not realise that – by speaking of his mother, of the dreariness and melancholy which had reigned in his house since she was taken ill, and of the incurable solitude in which his youth was going to waste – he was almost unconsciously preparing the ground to touch on the reason for his visit, and the explanation came from him all of a sudden and spontaneously, much more easily than he expected.

For a moment Erminia Corvaja was embarrassed, although she did smile with pleasure at the announcement; she clasped her hands together, avoided his eyes, and gathered her thoughts, as if considering some judicious reply. That moment of silence was very painful for Giulio Accurzi: he had expected that she would take the opportunity to speak to him about Mario Corvaja and her sister's state of mind; but now it was almost as though he wanted to speak of it first himself, merely in order to put an end to his suffering. And yet, what could he say to her? He already knew that she was pleased by his request. For the moment he had got over the most difficult stage. Certainly, he would have liked to feign surprise on learning that Agata had been, up until a few months ago, promised in marriage to another; but instead he feigned indifference, and replied to the sister:

'Yes... in fact, I knew...'

'Mere childishness, you understand,' Erminia hastened to add. 'It had been over for some time... All the same, you must understand, these things always leave a certain... how shall I put it?... perturbation in a girl's heart... Then, with time... Oh but now I am sure that Agata will be convinced that it was sheer foolishness, and not really worth thinking about... I, for my part, always foretold it of him... And it was, more than anything else, as you may well imagine, a matter of corresponding at a distance: my brother-in-law has always been away... first in Rome, then abroad.'

Giulio Accurzi was very pale as he listened to Erminia's words, with his lips frozen in a smile.

'I should like to hope… that it will not be any impediment… this broken engagement,' he stammered finally, 'at least as far as I am concerned.'

Erminia was happy to take on herself the task of telling her mother of this proposal of matrimony.

Her mother would then speak to Agata. He would have the reply within days. A little patience…

So they agreed. But once outside, Giulio felt himself embittered by an ill-defined anger and disheartened by a deep self-contempt.

Why?

8

Agata, still lying in bed, took note of the whiteness of her arms, still thin from her recent illness, and closely observed the tiny blue veins visible beneath the smooth skin.

Daylight was coming into the room through the green shutters, and on a shelf in a corner the night-light was dying away behind its transparent screen.

Signora Amalia had just left the room, and on Agata's brow the wrinkles left by the brief, unexpected dialogue with her mother were gradually smoothing out. Agata had never paid any attention to Giulio Accurzi, of whom her mother had spoken to her so hesitantly at first, and then with such interest. So that man was asking for her hand, knowing everything? And her mother and Erminia would be happy if she would consent to that marriage? Did they not know that for her another love was no longer possible now? Everything was over as far as she was concerned!

'Tell him no!' she had replied immediately. But then she had corrected herself, afraid that her mother would suspect that she was still thinking of 'that other one'. And she had said to her:

'Absoluitely not. Actually... look: as far as I'm concerned... do what you want... If you wish, you may tell him that I accept.'

And she had turned her back, pulling the covers over her shoulders.

But her mother had reproved her with some severity: 'No, not like this! It's not right, it's not honest. God forbid! An undertaking for life... Think of it! And when you have thought about it properly, we shall give your reply. As for love, have no doubt that that will come...'

'It will not come, it cannot come!' thought Agata, and at the same time she weighed against her depression her mother's wise advice and some reflections on her state. Giulio Accurzi was young, kind, rich. She was already several years past her first youth... And she had besides an affront to avenge, an affront to her as a woman – that abandonment which was still causing her so much grief.

'Well then,' asked Agata that evening of her mother. 'What have you decided?'

'Nothing, I told you... Have you thought about it?'

'Yes... I accept,' replied Agata.

Donna Amalia kissed her daughter with some emotion. And on the evening of the next day Giulio Accurzi went down for the first time into the home of the Sarni family.

Present at the introduction were Erminia Corvaja with her children, an old aunt of Agata's, bent, stout, yellow of complexion and wrinkled, with her pale eyes always full of tears, and her daughter Antonia, an old maid, who looked as though she were made of wood, and who never opened her mouth except to finish the sentences left in the air by her mother because of her difficulty in finding words. Mother and daughter were unsuitably dressed for the event and, although encumbered by their dresses, did not take their eyes off Agata.

The drawing-room was well lit, and strewn with fresh

flowers. Agata, who was very pale, looked now at her mother now at her sister, as though in a daydream. These two listened attentively to what was said by Giulio Accurzi, who preferred to speak to them; they frequently nodded their assent, and they smiled, possibly without grasping anything he was saying. The old aunt and her daughter observed the other four attentively and, from time to time, they sighed and exchanged a look of understanding.

Giulio Accurzi was clearly making every effort not to appear embarrassed, and Donna Amalia and her elder daughter came to his aid, as if by agreement. To begin with he talked of other matters, with a superfluity of words, interposing here and there broadly sensible maxims, but without any presumption, with the rather weary air of one who has taken the trouble now and then to think about life's ups and downs. Then he began to speak of his mother, and he was delighted, in front of Agata, to display all his filial affection, and his grief over the disaster which had overtaken his 'little old lady'.

'But then you will meet her…' he concluded, turning to Agata.

Agata lowered her eyes so as not to meet his glance, and held her breath for an instant.

The conversation lapsed. Giulio Accurzi's eyes wandered round the room, and stopped when they came to the open piano.

'You play a lot, don't you?' he asked Agata.

'Occasionally…' she answered, hesitantly, in a tiny voice.

'Go on, please play something…' Erminia hastened to add, and the old aunt and her daughter were quick to echo her. Donna Amalia looked at her daughter, who declined somewhat roughly, her cheeks rather red with shame.

'Please let me hear you play… if it isn't too much trouble for you,' Giulio insisted gently.

'I don't play very well… You will hear…' she said, rising and looking at him coldly.

He did not take his eyes off her for an instant while she was playing; and he admired her beautiful chestnut hair, so gracefully combed, the nape of her neck, her shoulders, her very slender waist... So she – so lovely, so adorable – had been rejected by that other man! So why had she?... He noticed that she was playing an old piece of music. Perhaps Mario Corvaja too had heard it played by those hands... Who knows? It might even have been a present from him. What was going through her mind at that moment?

When Agata finished playing, Giulio Accurzi was still troubled in his mind; nevertheless, he complimented the player, and talked about music...

'If I had been able to play, I might well have asked for nothing more from life... With music everything can be forgotten...'

He flushed as he said these last words. He suddenly remembered that recently Agata had been spending a large part of the day playing.

The conversation lapsed once more, and shortly afterwards he politely took his leave.

9

'She will come to love me!... she will come to love me!...' Giulio Accurzi repeated to himself as he left his fiancée's home.

He would win her over gradually, laying gentle and silent siege to her soul, searching in her eyes and on her lips for every desire, every hint of desire. He would overcome her with his submission, without hurting her feelings, and he would never try to penetrate the secrets of her heart directly; and so, with the mere breath of his passion, he was certain that his ardour would gradually bring back the colour and the former gaiety to that cold, pallid face. He would win her over...

He must, above all, be patient. Time, helped and nourished by his loving care, would, a little at a time, blot out from her heart the image of another man.

This is what he had come to think, keeping always present in his mind the image of Agata's cold bearing, as if to smother any strong impulse to jealousy. Although he suffered from it within himself, he preferred that she should be as she was, stiff and reserved with him.

From that first evening, in her presence, he felt he had lost that feeling of humiliation which he had suffered when he made the request to her sister. He guessed from Agata's welcome how she had been persuaded to accept, and the path he must follow in order to win her as soon as possible. But the more his thoughts, guided by the task he had set himself, abounded in love, the more he suffered in his heart, as though it were clenched in an iron vice by his impotent hatred of Mario Corvaja. This man might no longer be the lord of the unyielding fortress to which he was now laying loving siege; but he was the one who had left it so reserved and impenetrable! Giulio Accurzi sent flowers to Agata every morning, before she had risen from her bed: now a large bunch of loose roses, in a white silk kerchief, now a basket of gardenias, now a large straw hat, as worn by peasants, decorated with wild flowers... And he began to present her with his first gifts: rings, bracelets, brooches... She accepted them in a bewildered way, without sincere expressions of either gratitude or admiration; she took them from their rich cases with trembling hand, and left it to her mother to be profuse with expressions of wonder. Agata still addressed him formally.

'Not like this... I don't wish you to "express your gratitude" any more...' he eventually forced himself to say to her.

'Well then, thank you, my friend,' she said, inclining her head slightly and with scarcely a smile.

'That is better,' concluded Giulio frigidly. That enforced concession had not pleased him at all.

In the meantime he attended with alacrity to the furnishing of the house on the upper floor. Agata and Donna Amalia sometimes went with him to make purchases, and he chose everything on which her eyes rested for a moment in admiration.

Agata came with her mother to visit the invalid and the house which would soon welcome her as a bride. There was a great bustle there, for workmen were toiling away; it was only in the sick woman's room that the usual silence reigned. Giulio was present at this visit, and he did not take his eyes off his mother, as if afraid that she might greet her future daughter-in-law coldly.

In the last few days he had noticed a serious change in his mother. She, who was usually so resigned to her illness, was now continually lamenting, complaining about the noise the workmen made, impatient and curious to know what was happening in the other rooms... 'Giulio! Giulio!...' she kept calling out; and if he happened to be a little slow in coming, or showed the slightest irritation at the futility of her questions, she began to weep, to call on death 'in order not to be any more bother to anyone'. He bent over her and caressed her, and showed that he was afflicted almost to desperation...

'Just tell me... just tell me...' she managed to say in a vexed tone of voice. 'Listen, I've noticed already... I can see it... She makes you sad, doesn't she? Yes... yes... You are always sad because of her... I don't miss anything!'

'No, Mama... what are you thinking of?'

'Well then, it's because of me! Curse you, death! Why don't you come? What am I going to do here?'

However, she welcomed Agata with remarkable tenderness; she wanted Agata to sit next to her, she gazed at her for a long time, nodding her approval. Then she turned to her son.

'Giulio... Giulio, you give it to her... I can't...'

Giulio took from its case a splendid pearl necklace, that same one which reminded him of the vague figure of his father, and he handed it to Agata.

'Fasten it round her neck,' added the invalid, and she turned to look at her, nodding her approval.

Then, when Agata and her mother had gone, and Giulio had come back to her:

'You see?... Have I done the right thing?' she asked him, like a child.

'Yes, Mama, of course you have...'

'Oh well! As long as you go on being pleased with me...' she concluded, pursing her lips, and she began to weep silently.

10

On the eve of the wedding Giulio Accurzi did not close his eyes all night. Occupied with preparations for the ceremony, with fitting out the house, with clothing, with the necessary papers, he had in these last few days been living in a great rush, completely deaf to the contrary voices of his passion. He had wanted to hurry the day on, despite the short time allowed, with the obstinacy of a drunk. And now, look, he had succeeded: everything was ready... 'Tomorrow you'll have your ball and chain!' his friends had said to him, jokingly.

Between Agata and himself a sort of sympathetic understanding had been established. This at least was the illusion which he had created for himself during the three months of their engagement. Admittedly, Agata did not show him any love, and neither did he really lay claim to any. He seemed satisfied with the affectionate esteem and gratitude which she in her heart must have for him on account of the silence he had maintained over her past. In the evenings his mother, calm and serene, in order to leave them free to talk to each other, used to stay by the lamp, reading a big old holy book, *The Way to Heaven*; and the two of them, seated somewhat in the shade, far from the lamp, prudently contrived to avoid any confidence, any familiarity. One evening only, painfully embarrassed by a prolonged silence, he had allowed himself to be persuaded to ask her why she was always so sad...

'No, why should I be sad?' Agata had replied in a tiny voice, fiddling with the lace on her dress.

This was how he loved her; this was how he wanted to love her always.

Meanwhile dawn was breaking. The religious ceremony was to take place at eight in the morning, the civil ceremony at nine; then the newly-weds and their relatives would go into the country, where Giulio had been born, a few kilometres from the city. There the wedding breakfast had been prepared; and after it the relatives would return to the city, leaving the husband and wife alone in the splendid farmhouse. Few were invited: only their relatives and several close friends. That was how Agata had wanted it.

Giulio finished dressing, and he went to kiss his mother, who was still in bed.

'How handsome you are! Let me see you... You want to be off now? Yes, yes... go by all means. I bless you, and I hope you will be happy, my son!'

And her eyes, full of tears, accompanied him right to the door of the room.

'Send me up some of the sweets... don't forget!...'

Downstairs he was received by Cesare Corvaja, Erminia's husband, a dark, bearded colossus with large black eyes, a little awkward in his new, unaccustomed wedding clothes.

'Give me your hand, brother-in-law! We have not met... I am Cesare Corvaja.'

Giulio looked at him in bewilderment, extending his hand automatically. 'Mario's brother,' he was about to say, and he smiled coldly.

'This is a surprise, isn't it? What luck! I thought you were already married. Yes, I did! My wife wrote to me: "They are getting married very soon!" Good for them, I say, what a rush! Instead… I arrived yesterday evening. "Would you believe it?" Erminia said to me. "Agata is getting married tomorrow!" And so here I am… Agata, oh! she still knows nothing of my arrival… Erminia is in there, helping her to dress; I have been down in the dumps here… But look, what a surprise! Oh meanwhile, my congratulations…'

Giulio flushed bright red.

'Thank you,' he replied, extending his hand once again to the colossus, and he consulted his watch, pretending to be in a great hurry.

'But we must rush! Eight o'clock already…'

'Ah yes, the ladies! Hush! They're coming,' responded Cesare Corvaja, hiding himself behind the door as it opened.

Agata, very pale and already dressed for the ceremony, came in with Erminia. It was quite likely that she too had not closed her eyes all night.

'Good morning, my bride!' Giulio greeted her, pretending to be happy, in order to liven her up.

She gave him a sad smile.

'We're late… Mama is getting dressed…'

There was a loud burst of laughter from behind the door. Agata started and saw Cesare Corvaja in front of her.

'You… you here? But how? You frightened me! Oh, look! And hiding! But how?'

She reached both her hands to him, her face flushed with surprise, and she looked him up and down, laughing:

'Goodness, how ugly you are, got up like this!…'

'Excuse me... I beg you, Agata... it's already late,' observed Giulio with a forced smile.

'My husband!' exclaimed Agata, making a little face, as if determined to show herself happy in front of Cesare Corvaja.

Giulio had never seen her like this.

'Giulio, please, button this glove for me.'

The guests having arrived, they all went off on foot, in an orderly fashion, to the nearby church. Giulio knelt next to Agata on a hassock at the foot of the altar, and on the priest's command, he took Agata's frozen, trembling hand. He looked at her. It seemed to him that she was having difficulty in keeping back tears, and he squeezed her hand. Meanwhile the priest, in his nasal voice, was reading rapidly from a little book, and making signs over their heads with his hand; then he pronounced the customary formula:

'Yes,' said Giulio firmly, and waited anxiously for Agata's response. He noticed that she winced, and immediately regained control of herself, when he placed the wedding ring on her finger. They arose. The religious ceremony was over.

'Now for the other ceremony!' he whispered to his bride.

In the villa, during the meal, the high spirits were forced rather than spontaneous. Neither Agata nor Giulio, however hard they tried, could take a bite of food. Many healths were drunk and many good wishes expressed. Giulio felt exhausted, worn out by the day's emotion; he would have been glad on the one hand if all that desultory chatter and noise had not lasted much longer; and on the other hand, in his nervous exhaustion, he shrank from the thought that soon Agata and he would be left alone...

Meanwhile the weather, which up to then had been very fine, began gradually to cloud over; and so the guests, fearing some sudden downpour, decided to set off for the city immediately. In all the bustle of goodbyes Giulio hung about offering his thanks and shaking hands. He noticed Agata with her arms round her mother's neck and her face hidden: she was weeping.

'Cheer up... cheer up...' Erminia was saying to her quietly behind her mother.

Giulio turned away.

'You will see!... you will see... it is much easier than you might think...' someone was saying to him, shaking his hand at every word. He neither heard those words nor saw that his hand was in Cesare Corvaja's. Annoyed by the handshakes, he looked up at him and instinctively withdrew his hand. Cesare Corvaja went on talking to his nearest neighbour:

'Then, after so many years, one remembers! Now it seems that who knows what... But so it is! Life's like that...'

II

'Giulio!... Giulio!...' called Agata vivaciously, opening the door, and putting her head in, with her hair all loose. She was in a white dressing-gown, and held a comb in her hand. 'Come and see what a lovely little nanny-goat!...'

After the first night of rain and wind, the weather cleared up completely and became almost springlike; and so it continued for eight days.

Giulio, leaning on the railings of the balcony, was looking with knitted brows at the silent countryside under the rays of the warm sun. At the sound of Agata's voice he turned and, as if he expected that vivacity from her by now, he moved lazily away from the balcony, and followed Agata into another room.

'Look... Look... do you see her?' said Agata from the window, pointing to the avenue where a pretty little goat was playfully teasing an old and patient guard dog stretched out blissfully in the sun. 'Do you see her?... Just look!... look!...'

And Agata burst out laughing at every odd movement of the little creature left untethered in the fields.

'Poor old Turk!' was what Giulio said, with a melancholy smile: his sympathy was with the old dog which was being disturbed.

When she had finished combing her hair and dressing, they went out arm in arm into the countryside.

'What's the matter?' asked Agata. 'Have you nothing to say?'

'Do you notice how peaceful it is?' he replied.

Agata went on walking in silence, looking hard at the countryside. Her face, touched by a breath of fresh air, had taken on a lively colour, and her lips were glowing red once more. As she walked she pressed more and more closely against her companion, almost resting her head on the arm that supported her. From time to time she forced Giulio to stop: on that day she seemed overcome with admiration and wonder at every living thing on earth.

'Look!... look at these tiny flowers in February... how shy they are...'

Then he bent down to pick them.

'No, what are you doing? Poor things! They are not born for our sake... but for their own sake, on such a happy day...'

They came to the end of the field, which was marked by a low wall crowned and protected by brambles.

'Look! We could jump over that... Let's jump!' said Agata.

'No, Agata, you can't... Not in that dress... Let's go back instead...'

'Can't I? I'll show you...' Saying this, Agata let go of Giulio's hand as he tried to stop her, and she clambered onto the wall. Once she was up there her clothes, as she turned round, were caught in the brambles, and she was about to fall. Giulio ran up and caught and held her in his raised arms. She laughed heartily at the unfortunate outcome, and with her arms propped on Giulio's shoulders, she leant even further forward and tried to rub her forehead on his head...

'Wait, Agata! How are you going to get down now?'

'I shall support myself... you free me from the brambles... Then I will jump... This is mad!...'

'I told you it was...'

She started laughing again, even more heartily. Giulio could not find any way to disentangle the dress. Eventually, in his annoyance, he tore it slightly...

'Oh bother!' said Agata, jumping down, and then she looked at her dress to find out where it was torn.

'I'm sorry... What have I done?... I couldn't do anything else...' said Giulio, blushing. 'Shall we go back?'

Agata was no longer laughing. Walking along in silence, they went back to the house.

That evening Giulio suggested that they should return to the city the next day.

'What! must we go away so soon? The countryside is so beautiful... the freedom... You're bored already?'

'No! With you... bored?... But... you understand... my mother, poor thing...'

'Ah, of course!' sighed Agata. 'You're right... We'll go tomorrow.'

And the next day she rose at dawn, slipping out of the bed very carefully while he went on sleeping, pale and tired. She dressed as well as she could without making any noise, and left the warm room where the lamp was still burning and the first thin streaks of dewy dawn were streaming in through the cracks in the blinds. Outside, the birds were already singing; and, as if responding to their invitation, she went out, wrapped in a light shawl, shivering in the fresh dawn breeze.

She wandered through the fields, which were bathed in dew, saw the sun rise and, her concern for the flowers giving way to a loving thought, she gathered as many of them as she could;

34

she came back into the house and, throwing open the door of the warm room, she burst in, laden with fragrant flowers. Giulio awakened with a start, and she threw onto his face, into his hands, and onto his breast all the flowers she had gathered.

'No... no... what are you doing?... They're all drenched...'

'It's the dew! I am bringing the spring into your bed! Stir yourself, you poor thing!'

He drew her to him in an impulse of tenderness, and he clutched her tightly, for a long while, breathing in from her neck and her dress the morning country breeze.

'Why didn't you wake me sooner? We could have gone out together early... We'll take these flowers with us when we go back into the city, as a souvenir...'

'Yes! In half an hour they will be dead!' she exclaimed, gathering them up. And they both fell silent, he as though cast down by the imminent death of the flowers, and she by their imminent departure for the city.

12

'Come here... Sit down. That's right! Now let me take your hands. You must tell me what's wrong.'

'Nothing, Agata... What do you think is wrong?'

'That's not true! I can see that you are not happy...'

'I'm very happy! Since I began to love you when you still did not love me...'

'But I didn't know you then!'

'Yes... yes... that's true. But, truly, were you never aware...'

'Never, I swear to you.'

'I do know that at that time you...'

'Please, Giulio, don't talk to me about that time...'

'Why not? Oh, that's a fine thing! Perhaps you think I'm jealous… Not in the least! If you are mine now, completely mine…'

'Why then…'

Agata's question was interrupted by a flood of tears. Giulio hastened to reply:

'It's all in your mind! You persist in believing that I am not happy, while… One really can't be laughing all the time! And you, in your condition…'

Agata attributed the sudden melancholy into which Giulio seemed to have fallen to jealousy for her past love. 'I was so cold towards him at first!' she thought. 'Perhaps he thinks that my feelings for him are only ones of affectionate esteem and gratitude for his silence, as before. But now…' And she made every effort to show her love for him in every possible way, particularly with cheerfulness, to blot out the first impression of coldness which he must have received from her previous attitude. At the same time in her heart she cursed the memory of that other man, which was even now coming back, she thought, to disturb her peace. But did Giulio believe in those manifestations of love? Sometimes it almost seemed to her that he was secretly vexed by her cheerfulness, as if he did not wish to see her so affectionate and contented. How coldly he had pronounced the words, 'If you are mine now, completely mine…' 'But what can be troubling him now?' she wondered that evening, all in a flutter, while he was out of the house, and she – in the same room as the invalid who was always lying back in the armchair with her eyes shut – was getting the clothes ready for the baby. It was now five months since the wedding, and she had been pregnant for two. Giulio certainly never did anything reprehensible; and yet in her heart Agata reproached him for all that he did not do. She felt that he really did not wish to fall short of any promise of love which he had made; but that was a cold fulfilment of his vows, and nothing more... Yes... yes... As if he had been cheated in his expectations! Who knows...

From time to time the sick woman uttered a sigh like a lament, letting her head fall onto her other shoulder. Agata, who was by the lamp, stopped sewing and looked at her closely in the half-light.

'Do you want anything, Mama?'

'Nothing.'

At other times, raising her eyes, she met the cold glance of her mother-in-law fixed upon her.

'Are you still sewing?'

'Yes, Mama.'

'It must be late... Giulio is not back...'

'Let him stay out. What would he do here with us?'

'But I would like to be put to bed...'

'Shall I call the maid?'

'No... no... No one knows how to look after me as he does... Are you two always so much at odds with each other? Now he makes me wait so long, every evening... He used to be so punctual...'

'I am waiting for him just as you are, Mama... We're not cross with each other...'

Already Giulio was beginning to feel a little disappointed; excuses and disputes followed as he tried to prove to her that he had not failed her. And indeed he did not fail her openly, as Agata would have preferred. So in the end he killed off for ever the last rare smiles and tender cheerfulness which had lingered on her lips.

13

As if temporarily attracted by the sadness which had come over Agata, Giulio stayed at home as he had been accustomed to, and he began once more to lavish on her his old acts of affection and kindness.

'You are already regretting that you are mine?'

'No, Giulio... I'm suffering on your behalf!'

And little by little she, diffident to begin with, but encouraged by his endearments, became cheerful again. But it did not last long. Giulio fell back into vexation, and then into boredom.

The little garden down below, at the foot of the house, had been left to itself, and there were no more flowers. Even its owner was not as he had been once.

Agata, in order not to upset her mother, would take the carriage and go to see her sister, for advice or because she needed comforting.

'All men are like that,' Erminia said to her. 'Fire before the wedding, and ashes afterwards.'

But Agata was not convinced by that.

'No... no... There must be something more to it! It may be my destiny... Loved when I do not love; not loved when I love. And it is the second attempt...'

'You're making it too hard for yourself! It will pass... You see me? Already I am accustomed...'

'You are happy!' sighed Agata.

'I, happy? I never have my husband with me!'

'That's exactly it! Ah! so it seems to you a fine thing to have him always at home, sad and bored, without knowing why? You cannot understand what I suffer! You have grown accustomed to a peaceful life, waiting whole months for your husband; you look after your little ones; you don't concern yourself with anything else... When he returns there is a whole week of joy... Your love never has time to get tired...'

'But you believe that Giulio does not love you?'

'I don't know... I don't know... Meanwhile, you see me...'

And in her desolation Agata pointed out to her sister her condition.

One day Giulio, sitting at the end of a meal reading his newspaper as usual, suddenly gave vent to a strange, noisy laugh.

'What's happening?' asked Agata.

'Look... look here...' he exclaimed, continuing to laugh and putting the open newspaper in front of her.

'What?'

'Here... read it... Notice the signature!'

Agata looked, and she went very pale. Giulio did not stop laughing. It was a poem by Mario Corvaja entitled *The Desertion*.

'Read it! Don't you see? He has had it printed here, in this paper, so that you would read it...The rogue! He's really in torment, poor fellow! Read it! Art has disappointed him... the ideal has left him... and you have returned to his heart... He loves you once more! You hear what he says?

'If you could only see my burning love!

'Well then, you see what you are doing, my poor Agata?'

Agata let the paper fall from her hands, and looked at Giulio in stupefaction. Then he bent over her; he embraced her and clutched her head to his breast, kissing her hair again and again.

'Giulio, please!...'

'Oh, I'm sorry... I was not thinking... I've hurt you?'

He knelt in front of her, took her hands in his, and went on speaking endearingly, gazing into her eyes:

'I've taken a fancy to that idiot... He's sorry for it now, you see? Leaving you, who are so lovely... so good...'

Agata smiled sadly, somewhat confused.

'Lovely? Even now?...'

Giulio rose, annoyed by the interruption.

'I haven't hurt you, have I?'

14

Sudden shadows were stretching out over the city, and rain seemed imminent that evening. Already the horse had a presentiment of it, neighing under the tall rustling trees as it drew the carriage along the avenue taking Agata to the seaside suburb where Erminia lived.

Agata was on the point of telling the coachman to turn back. But Cesare Corvaja was arriving that evening from America, and Erminia had invited her and Giulio to the house.

After the incident with the newspaper, another change had come over Giulio. Now he no longer cut her affectionate reproofs short with a bored exclamation; indeed, they seemed to please him, and he smiled in response, with an air of superiority and condescension.

'It's all right, all right... you'll get what you want... This evening I'll be home ten minutes earlier than usual... That's what you want, isn't it?...'

He was delighted to feel himself loved by her, and happy in the knowledge that she was suffering because of him. 'Does he want revenge?' wondered Agata. 'As if at that time I wanted to make him suffer! But I did not know him!...' Moreover Giulio continued to show himself patient under everything, lending an ear to the reproofs; as if he really had a right to act as he was acting; and as if she in addition ought to thank him for his ostentatiously benign tolerance. And he demanded from her a greater care in her dress. He did not wish to see her so untidy at home…

'Women are all the same! As soon as they've got a husband they don't take any more care of their appearance. As though he were no longer worth the trouble!… The poor husband should not have eyes for anything any more, he should submit to his bondage, whether it is pleasant or not…'

And Agata had anxiously begun to dress with more care in order to please him, discouraged though she was in front of her mirror to see her listless face and her disfigured body.

The carriage halted in front of Erminia's house, and Agata descended from it slowly and heavily.

When she reached the top of the steps, she could hardly stand and she was panting, with her eyes half closed.

She tugged at the bell-pull, and waited a long time with her pale hand on the door and her forehead resting on her hand.

Was no one coming to open the door?

At last the door opened.

'Who is it?' asked a voice which made her heart miss a beat.

Mario Corvaja put his head out a little to look:

'Agata!' he exclaimed, drawing back as though afraid.

She remained on the threshold, with her hand against the door. The hall was in darkness. 'He's here? How can he be here?' After a moment's indecision Agata entered. Inside, there were no lamps lit in the rooms. At the end of the last room the glass in the balcony revealed an ashen glimmer from the sea.

Mario followed her right into that room.

'Erminia?' she asked anxiously, holding onto the laid table in the middle of the room.

'She's not here,' replied Mario, and then suddenly, as Agata made a movement, he added, 'No, no! You stay here; I'll go…

Sit down… Erminia is at the quayside, with the children… The ship's already in port…'

Agata let herself fall onto a dining chair. 'And so why doesn't he go away?' she thought, breathing with difficulty once silence had fallen again; and in the dark she felt him looking at her, cast down and surprised to find her in that condition.

He could not make up his mind whether to go or to speak. He had his face hidden in his hands. In both of them perhaps, in the emotion of the moment, the tumultuous memory of other times had reawakened.

They could hear the sound of the sea nearby, and the room was steadily growing darker.

Suddenly Agata stood up, resolutely.

'I'll go,' repeated Mario, taking his hands away from his face.

And after a short pause, he added, almost in a stammer:

'Forgive me, Agata… for the wrong… which I did you…'

'No wrong…' she said dully.

Mario came to himself outside the house, without knowing how he had come to be there, and he went off automatically to the quay. Halfway there he met his brother, with his two children in his arms, and with Erminia on one side of him and the maid on the other.

'Here he is!' exclaimed Cesare, when he saw him. 'Give me a kiss! I can't embrace you… how are you? You've gone thin, haven't you?'

'I'm going into the country, to Papa's place, to recover somewhat… I'm leaving tomorrow morning,' replied Mario, almost dazed. And then, turning to Erminia, he added, 'Agata is here… she has come to see you…'

'Agata?' asked Erminia anxiously. 'You have seen her?…'

'Yes… She's waiting for you!'

'Poor Agata!' said Cesare.

'Unrecognisable!' Mario pronounced each syllable separately, almost to himself.

'Well, naturally! Apart from herself she's carrying...' resumed Cesare, and he added, smiling and shifting the children in his arms: 'While I am carrying three!'

When they arrived home, they found there Giulio Accurzi, who had just come, and Agata in the same position in which Mario had left her.

The room was still dark.

'Hurrah!' cried Giulio, rather out of character, turning to Erminia and striking a match. 'Is this how we ought to welcome a husband who has come from America? Light all the lamps! We want to see his face!'

Cesare kissed him, and introduced his brother.

'It's a great pleasure!...' exclaimed Giulio effusively, shaking Mario's hand. 'I used to know him... that is, by sight... Oh yes. He comes from Rome, doesn't he? He's a happy man who can live up there, in freedom... Bountiful Rome! And the pretty girls?' he added softly, with a wink.

Mario, who was very pale, looked him in the face. Shaking his head he answered:

'Yes! Bountiful Rome... a wide desert...'

'What! What are you saying? A wide desert!'

'For me...'

'Ah, for you, perhaps... I'd like to be in your shoes... Without a wife, of course! A wife is a serious consideration, when one is young, like us. Isn't that so, Cesare?'

His eyes were shining, and his voice was quivering, like that of someone with a high fever.

Agata was looking at him as if she were every moment afraid that he would fly into a rage.

'You're looking at me...' Giulio suddenly turned to her, laughing. 'But it is the truth, dear! It is the truth!...'

And as he looked at his wife only one thought, an almost incredible one, suddenly disturbed his sad pleasure at being hated by Mario Corvaja just as Mario Corvaja had once been hated by him: her condition did not allow him to achieve a complete victory, since by this stage Agata could perhaps no longer inspire in that man any torments of jealous love.

The Signorina

'Oh, in the end, what will be, will be!' said Lucio Mabelli to himself, shrugging his shoulders.

He rose from his chair; and from the table, which was cluttered with papers scattered higgledy-piggledy and piles of books, he gathered together the dozen pages onto which he had carelessly thrown down his usual column for a daily newspaper on art and life in society, and started to dress in order to go out.

'What will be, will be! Gently now... And that imbecile Marzani?'

Yes, an imbecile all right; but how could he forget, all of a sudden like this, the many and not insignificant favours received from Marzani on a number of difficult occasions?

'Oh, yes... it's all right! it's all right!'

He flung the towel onto a chair, and snorted in irritation.

Look at what he had come down to! And always humiliated! Who had he worked for and why had he worked for so many years? How had his work been rewarded? Neither fame nor money – at the age of thirty-four! Who had played fair with him? No one... And must he now play fair with other people? Ah, he would not be so foolish! Be patient a while, but not so foolish...

'Marzani has not managed to speak? All the worse for him! What fault is it of mine?'

But however hard he tried to find excuses and even tried to be unfair, a tiny pang of remorse would not allow him to overcome that internal agitation, that anxiety in his mind. Did he not know that his friend Tullo Marzani was in love with Signorina Giulia Antelmi? He had it from Marzani's own mouth.

'Yes, it's true! But who could have supposed...'

Ah, for goodness' sake, suppose!... Ought he not to have expected this outcome from the signorina? Come on, come on, to be honest, had he too not paid some court to her?... But yes, without meaning to, you understand! He had trifled, as one does with a spirited signorina, but that was all! In all conscience, however, had he not been aware that Giulia Antelmi was beginning to have a taste for that trifling? That too might have been foreseen! These days, with such a shortage of husbands... And so, let's hear, what should he have done?... Straight away start keeping his distance from that house... Oh yes! And why not go the whole hog and become a monk?

Besides, even he could not now fully account for what had happened between himself and Signorina Antelmi.

Meanwhile he snorted once more, and stayed for a while with his arms propped on the bed in front of the shirt which he was going to put on that evening. Yesterday's scene came into his mind with cruel accuracy. That cursed trip to San Paolo! That stupid Marzani! He was the one who had proposed the trip...

Curiously, it was of him, of Marzani, that he and Signorina Giulia, arm in arm, had been speaking as they were coming back from Tre Fontane to San Paolo, while the day died in a blazing pallor. What a day! He had forgotten all the injustice in the world, and his wretched existence made up of vexation and renunciation, and his unfulfilled dreams... He had felt that his soul was light and free, and his heart contented and full of joy, in the constant severity of the wintry air, on that glorious day, without a cloud on the clear blue sky throbbing with light. Together they had, quite involuntarily, distanced themselves from the others, from her parents and from Marzani, who, as usual, was explaining to everyone the most obvious things in the world, things which were already clear enough in themselves.

Lucio maintained that he knew the signorina's secret; she on the other hand maintained that he did not, that it was impossible that he should.

'And if, for example, I were to tell you that he told me… he?'

'Who do you mean by "he"?'

'A man, probably! By "he" I mean that lucky mortal…'

She had begun to laugh, without realising at all that with his free hand he was pressing the little gloved hand that was hanging on his right arm.

There really was some ambiguity here. He did seriously believe that Signorina Giulia's secret consisted of her flirtation with Marzani.

'Isn't it Tullo Marzani?'

'Marzani? Goodness no! Are you serious? Leave him alone, poor old Marzani!'

'If this is so, I certainly won't leave *you* in peace! He told me a little story, I don't know…'

'Marzani?'

'Yes, Marzani, months ago…'

'Sheer imagination! What do you want me to say?'

'Ah, it's not possible, is it? And he… Now you're trying to make fun of me. Go on, we understand… If Tullo has spoken to me about you in such a way that…'

'Well? Please thank him on my behalf.'

'He's really in love. Head over heels!'

'With me? Oh, for goodness' sake!'

'Did you really not know?'

'Oh, for a long time…'

And she had begun to laugh again, like a little scamp. But now he wanted to know the secret.

'Tell me who it is really, if it's not Marzani…'

'Do I have to tell you? You're being a little presumptuous, it seems to me…'

'Don't worry, I will find out!'

'You really don't know?'

And as she said this, she had suddenly become serious, and

struck him twice in the face, lightly, with the long black glove which she was holding in her right hand.

At that he gave a start, realising at long last the false position into which, forgetful for a moment of himself and everyone else, he had let himself be drawn by his unaccustomed light-hearted mood, by his vanity being tickled.

The silence which succeeded those two blows of the glove was now, in his memory, weighing very heavily on his heart. Ah, that silence had compromised him more than any thought-less sentence that had slipped out of his mouth that day, more than the signorina's rash action, more than his hand, which was squeezing, almost without realising it, her hand.

'God, how stupid! how stupid!'

What she added then, in an effort to break the silence, had resulted in his utter confusion.

'Perhaps you'd like to know… "my old secret"? I'll tell you! It's not worth taking the trouble to find out… It's over and done with…'

And from her tone of voice and the expression in her eyes it was abundantly clear why she was about to reveal 'her old secret' to him. Without doubt the signorina supposed that he wished to know it because he was jealous of her past, as tended to happen with some exacting suitors. And she wanted to re-assure him.

'I can even tell you the name. In fact, he's no longer here, he's left Rome. I'll even tell you where he's gone to: to Milan. He has written to me twice; I have never replied to him. Can you still not guess?'

And after a short pause:

'His name is Antonio… an ugly name, eh?'

What came to his lips was a foolish, banal remark, accom-panied by a frozen, stupid smile: 'Do you expect me to believe that?'

'Why not? Yes! Antonio Arnoldi.'

Antonio Arnoldi? Him? Was it possible? He could not imagine a more unpleasant surprise! And she was the one giving it to him! He gazed at her in stupefaction, almost offended by the revelation. Arnoldi? Was it possible? That disagreeable fellow?

Arnoldi's image flashed into Lucio's mind – tall, dark, with curly hair and beard, his eyes black and flashing, his lips red, vigorous, and scornful.

'Now what's come over you?' Giulia Antelmi asked him, noticing how upset he was by the surprise.

'Ah, signorina!… I am amazed…'

'At what?'

'At you, if you'll pardon me…'

'I shall explain… Wait a second! I have known Arnoldi…'

Oh no, he would have preferred to believe that she did not know him at all, or at least did not really know what kind of man he was, because otherwise… Yes, that was it! He understood very well: we can all fall in love with someone who is, let us say, ugly, but intelligent, or with a bad lot who is good-looking… Now, that Arnoldi was certainly no Adonis; he certainly was no Aristotle either…

'What has Aristotle got to do with it?' she had interrupted him with a smile. 'Let me speak…'

Signorina Giulia did not know what Arnoldi was like. Strange, wasn't it? And yet so it was! She had known him a long time ago. She was a girl, and he was a lad! She used to go to school accompanied by Aia – an old woman in the neighbourhood – and Arnoldi, he too with textbooks and exercise books under his arm, followed her at a distance. He escorted her in this way for a year: she was thirteen years old at that time. One day the old woman was late picking her up from school. Giulia stayed waiting by the main gate, stretching her neck to see if she was coming, but she was not! Instead, he came up to her, the little gentleman, with the suggestion of a moustache on his lips by now. He addresses her formally; he says, 'Signorina...' Just imagine! She was still in short skirts, reaching just to the calf... And he plucked up the courage to tell her that he loved her, there and then, in such terms... such terms... She ran away, without replying, right into the school's entrance hall. The next day the escorting at a distance recommenced. And, well, she, naughty girl, who knows? Perhaps she gave him to understand, yes... that she had understood, in short... There was nothing more. When their happy schooldays were over, when she had really become a signorina, she had seen him again four or five times (she did not know how many exactly), at very long intervals, in the houses of common friends. Just one time, however, on one of these occasions (don't ask!) Arnoldi, taking advantage of a moment's carelessness (which was quite innocent, notice!) and supposing that she had kept a little apart for his sake, had come to her very politely, and had said to her that he had never forgotten his schoolgirl in the past, and said that now he would think seriously of the signorina. She went as red as a beetroot, and went away without having the strength to reply to him as she should have done... What he was like now, after all these years, Signorina Giulia really did not know. She had never been near him. For her, Arnoldi had always been that daring little lad who had accompanied her every morning right to the gates of the school. She had thought of him in this way, perhaps because he was thinking of her... And that was all.

Her account certainly gave an impression of sincerity. Was it not in fact a rather endearing little adventure? Giulia Antelmi had put that to him. But he, of course, in order to make up in some way for his previous ill-humour, had then shown such indifference clothed in kind words and wise advice... In his heart, however, he would have preferred it a thousand times over if Signorina Giulia had said to him: 'I loved your friend,

Tullo Marzani,' and not that Arnoldi, that Arnoldi for whom he felt such an instinctive, inexplicable antipathy! In fact, if he had not been afraid of compromising himself still further, he would have expressed to her, with some warmth in his gestures and his voice, his great disgust, and revealed everything bad which he knew about Arnoldi. As it was, he had confessed 'quite frankly' that that man was not only not worthy of her love (that would have been an enormity!), but not worthy even of the remotest interest.

'But whatever has he done?'

'Who knows?... How he managed to live I don't know. There is someone who knows, and also goes about saying it quite openly. I, however, wouldn't let myself repeat it to you.'

'He has done some horrible things?'

'Well!...'

Besides, Giulia Antelmi did not now need to know at all. The worse for him, for Arnoldi!

'The worse for me!' was what Lucio Mabelli was thinking, finding himself already in the street, on the way to the newspaper's printing office.

2

'One... two... three... four... five... six... seven...'

Signor Carlo Antelmi was standing on a chair by the door of the drawing-room, which was decorated with certain pretensions to elegance that only made the poverty of the available means more obvious. With his finger he was turning the hands of a large old pendulum-clock in a cabinet on the wall. After turning them right round once on the clock-face he waited to see if the mechanism, which had been striking the wrong hour, would now get it right. Seven again, curse it!

'Who is it?'

Someone entered the room; and Signor Carlo, tall and gaunt and wearing a rather crumpled dressing-gown, with a travelling-cap on his head and a large woollen kerchief round his neck, turned round on the chair, bending down towards the door, to see who it was.

'It's me, Signor Carlo... Am I disturbing you?' asked Tullo Marzani uneasily, as he came in.

Signor Carlo hurried down from the chair.

'Signor Marzani! Not at all! Come in! No trouble at all... How are you? *You* should excuse me for being in this state...'

'I'm sorry, it is a little early in the day to pay a visit; but, look, I had this sheet of music which Signorina Giulia wanted to see; and so, since I was passing, I came up. That's all! I know the signorina plays in the mornings, and so...'

'That's too good of you... too good...' repeated Signor Carlo, bowing and smiling in his pleasure.

But Tullo Marzani felt the need to explain himself more clearly: the maid had been determined that he should come in whether he wanted to or not; but he would have preferred to leave the music and go away immediately, without disturbing anybody...

With one excuse or another, Tullo Marzani often made these sudden appearances in the Antelmi household, the result no doubt of meditations and opinions offered during some troubled nights, during which, worn out at last by a long period of continual indecision, he had felt the need to decide to do something. Should he, or should he not, take a wife? One opinion was that he should, and another that he should not. Was Signorina Antelmi suitable for him, or not? As far as her looks went, yes, certainly; everyone thought her a lovely girl, but she was a little eccentric, a little too free and easy; some people... She was no housewife; she preferred to read novels... 'That's bad... bad...'

one little voice said to him inside, but immediately another voice replied: 'You won't want to banish your wife to the kitchen!' – Pish! – Signorina Antelmi had no dowry – 'All the better! She will be under more of an obligation to you...' suggested another voice in his mind. 'Oh no!' admonished another. 'You, with your income, can aspire a little higher...'

But ultimately poor Marzani, devoid by that time of any criteria or sense of judgement, liked Signorina Giulia very much. And so finally, all of a sudden, he took the decision to ask for her hand in marriage. 'I shall take her, and let's say no more about it!'

He got out of his bed, which had become an instrument of torture for him, and with shadows under his eyes through lack of sleep, without his usual ruddy complexion, he made a plan, looked for a believable excuse, and went off to the home of the Antelmi family.

Here it seemed that everyone was always waiting for him with open arms, Signor Carlo, Signora Erminia, even the maid; even if they were rather tired by now, to tell the truth, by the very long wait, especially Signora Erminia, who nevertheless took care not to let her impatience show.

The worst of it was that, without realising it, he had let slip the opportunity when Signorina Giulia, disappointed by Arnoldi's departure for Milan, constrained by the poverty of her home, and thinking herself misunderstood by her family, would perhaps have accepted his proposal of matrimony.

Now, in order to keep the peace with her mother, she had to make an effort to conceal the antipathy which Marzani inspired in her; and meanwhile she had turned to Mabelli and held onto him, like a rock on which she did not really feel very safe, in the shipwreck of her hopes. She knew that Mabelli was in no position to take a wife, but she depended on his brilliance and flirtatiousness.

Lucio, from the day when he had let himself be ambushed, as it were, by his own heart, quite against the grievous demands of reason and necessity, had no longer been able to oppose Giulia's assumptions openly, and for her they had gradually become certainties, on account of his silence and his compliance. He thought: 'Can I say to her: "You know what, signorina? I was joking that day; don't think that I am really in love with you…" I certainly can't say that to her. She will understand that by herself, by my behaviour…'

These notions, meanwhile, remained intentions merely. In reality, Giulia Antelmi was catching him in the coils of her mischievous wit, wrapping him unawares in the momentary perturbation of a surreptitious effusion of affection; and so he always came out of her house abashed, annoyed with himself, with a restless feeling of unease and an ever clearer consciousness of the false position in which he had placed himself.

Why did he not speak? Did he not feel in his heart that loyalty, honesty, and duty towards his friend, whose secret he possessed, and whom he was betraying, were commanding him to speak? Was it loyal, was it honest to deceive by his silence a signorina whose age did not allow any further delay in aimless light-hearted flirtations? She was already twenty-five, as Lucio knew. It was true that she only looked twenty or perhaps twenty-one; yes, and she was beautiful too, and so witty! What a disaster that she had no dowry! Lucio would have been a fool to remain indifferent to all his resolutions against the temptations of marriage. He admitted it to himself, perhaps to stifle his conscience which was disgusted by his behaviour. Had he not gone so far as to allow himself to be kissed by her? And had he not several times heard Giulia pillory Marzani in front of him? And he had even smiled at her sharp tongue, a little embarrassed it is true, but without being able to say a word in defence of his friend, whom he was betraying in this way, almost without wanting to…

He did not speak, he who should have spoken, and meanwhile he even blamed Marzani for it, since he could not make up his mind once and for all to ask for Giulia's hand, and so get him out of his fix. Had he been able to persuade Marzani to do that, he, meanwhile, could have cleared things up candidly with Signorina Giulia. It would be difficult and painful, he had no doubt; but it was all the more necessary…

So, one morning, he paid a visit to Marzani.

'Oh, Lucio! How are you?' said Marzani, receiving him in his study, which was always neat and tidy, and arising from his writing-desk.

'You are busy?'

'Heaps of things!… Heaps!… I swear I can't go on any longer.'

'All right then, let's go out. The weather's fine, and we're not working. Let's go out.'

'Have you something to say to me?'

'No. We'll go for a walk. We'll discuss things…'

'Yes, but… these papers?'

'Forget them. You can look at them later. Hurry up, we're off!'

Tullo Marzani always had heaps of things to do, or at least he liked to believe he had, and he told everyone he had. The truth was that from time to time some friends would shower him with some legal bother, which he used to dispatch with the greatest care, often submitting a bill for his expenses however. There was nothing else!

'Just tell me, have you been dreaming?' began Lucio Mabelli, once they were in the street. 'What the devil did you tell me about Signorina Antelmi… about yourself?'

'Ah, have you spoken to her?' exclaimed Marzani, opening his eyes wide, and looking puzzled.

'No, no! What an idea! But listen, there is an ambiguity…'

'You have spoken to Signorina Giulia about me! Tell the truth…'

'The answer is no. You're a strange person!… It was she rather who spoke to me…'

'About me?'

'Certainly not.'

'Well then?'

Tullo turned pale. He looked at Lucio. That air of indifference with which Mabelli had come to invite him out, the affected lightness with which he was speaking of something which was so important to him, made him suddenly suppose that his friend wanted first to hide from him, and then gradually prepare him to hear some unpleasant news.

'I don't understand…' he added. 'Who did the signorina speak to you about?'

Lucio began to feel uneasy under Marzani's puzzled gaze; but suddenly he turned against his friend the bitter remorse which was biting him now more than ever. It always happened like that with him: his remorse turned into irritation, and then he attributed his fault to whoever for one reason or another had driven him to commit it…

'Now don't start…' he replied. 'Nothing has happened! Stay calm. Anyway, the fault's yours, my dear…'

'What? But I…'

'Let me speak! You… you have no right to complain about anyone. No, because you are indecision personified. Do you understand? You propose this, you propose that, you talk, you make believe that everything's done, oh yes! And then you do nothing. Admit it.'

'Excuse me, but I…'

'But you what? Isn't it true that you have spoken to me about Giulia Antelmi? Isn't it true that you told me that you liked her, that you meant to marry her, that she too was secretly

58

thinking about you? Oh! And since you confided all that to me, five months, at least, have gone by... I know! Do not interrupt me... Five months! At that time you looked as though you were ready to take this step. What have you done up to now? What have you achieved? Nothing! And now you grumble...'

'But what is all this to you? What has happened? For heaven's sake, may I know?...'

'What? Nothing, up to now; but if you continue to delay... What does it matter to me? Look, I don't understand you! If I were in your shoes... Single, rich, without worries, except those which you positively ask for. Will you tell me what more you want? Ah, love! And you would like to have it like this, without putting yourself out, without saying anything? What are you still waiting for? Are you waiting for women to throw themselves round your neck the moment they see you?'

'That is something I've never expected...' said Tullo, mortified. 'But I still don't understand why you have come to make this speech to me, today... Look, I have a suspicion... I don't want to tell you, but...'

Lucio was rather disconcerted, and he turned to look at his friend.

'You want me to tell you frankly?' asked Marzani. He was embarrassed, and he tried to smile first, as if to soften his words. 'Frankly, I don't blame you... Listen, I... yes, I am willing to swear that Signorina Giulia believes... or at least it has seemed to me, rather! yes, she believes... in short, that you are paying court to her... just a little, you know!'

'Are you mad?' exclaimed Lucio. 'Me? Paying court?'

'You are not, there's no question of it, I know! I am saying that she perhaps believes it...'

'Oh, but she... can believe... what she wants to... I...' responded Lucio. The words took his breath away, and he concealed his agitation in a burst of laughter. 'I pay court! That would be the day! And yet, yes, I can assure you that I have everything it takes to be the ladies' favourite... Come off it, come off it, don't say silly things, and don't make me say them!... When I think, and I do at times, that I am as old as I am, and that I happen to live as I do, after so many... That's enough of that! Better not to speak of it. You are complaining, you have the gall to complain!... That's enough of that; listen... I was telling you that there is an ambiguity, wasn't I... Well then, just tell me: do you know Arnoldi? Antonio Arnoldi.'

'Yes, why? I know him by sight... Wait a minute. I saw him only yesterday evening.'

'Here? In Rome? No, that's not possible!' said Lucio. The sudden surprise made him change his tone.

'I think I saw him...'

'Come off it, you must be mistaken... It's not possible!'

'And I'm telling you that's who it was. Got up like Beau Brummel in fact... but then, an upstart... yes, with his usual air...'

'He's come back from Milan?'

'It looks like it.'

'To do what?'

'Um!' said Tullo. 'Who knows? Probably to start again doing what he used to do...'

Lucio was not listening to what Marzani said. 'To do what?' he repeated to himself, as if he wanted at all costs to find a connection between that unexpected return and what he was about to say to Marzani.

He was upset, and became lost in a mass of suppositions.

Meanwhile, Tullo went on backbiting Arnoldi without any embarrassment.

'Perhaps,' he said, 'he hasn't been able to go on living even in Milan; and so he has returned to his old loves...'

Lucio was annoyed by this.

'You're mistaken,' he said, to shut him up. 'Arnoldi, my friend, has found a very good position in Milan, in the Ritter Bank. He has a good mind, you don't realise, and a will of iron... He is rather debauched, or at least he was.'

'He certainly was!' exclaimed Marzani with a laugh.

'Well, you're laughing, and I'm telling you... What a coincidence! You are in love with Signorina Giulia, aren't you? Now you ought to know that for quite a while she was in love with Antonio Arnoldi...'

'With him?' shouted Tullo, and he came to a halt.

'Nothing bad, you understand!' Lucio hastened to add, in order to correct the bad impression which his words, uttered in irritation, had made on his friend. 'Nothing bad... A foolish girlish flirtation, yes, girlish... They used to go to school together, imagine! And it's been over a long time...'

'Is this the ambiguity?' asked Tullo. He was still bewildered.

'Yes. I repeat, there is nothing to worry about...'

And he told him briefly everything that Signorina Giulia had told him about this girlish affair, and what he had replied and said about Arnoldi. Then, when he thought that his friend was completely reassured, he took leave of him and left him, as usual, hotfoot.

'Well, well; we'll speak of it again some other time. Now, let me be off...'

'I'll come with you.'

'No. I have to see Count Rivoli on behalf of Signor Carlo Antelmi. Poor man! We'll see if it is possible to get him that post of secretary to the Count. I have hopes...'

'I hope it turns out all right,' said Tullo, shrugging his shoulders, with his thoughts still full of Arnoldi. 'I'll go back to my papers then...'

'And to your indecision!' added Lucio, as he went away.

And he thought to himself: 'Now more than ever! I was wrong to reveal *the old secret* to him, all of sudden like that. I had started to prepare him very well. But that news... What can it be that Arnoldi has come to Rome to do?'

3

Signor Antelmi was waiting impatiently for the reply from Count Rivoli, and as he wandered about the house he was praising Mabelli to himself: he seemed to have gone to some trouble to obtain that secretarial post for him.

He, like Signora Erminia, had a blind faith in Lucio: they had not the slightest suspicion that he might have an ulterior motive in lending a hand to help them on every occasion as much as he could. Lucio for his part was able to confer his favours with such superiority, and he knew so well how to conceal himself behind an appearance of changeable vivacity, that indeed he gave no occasion for suspicion.

As for Signorina Giulia, to her parents she had always been like a closed book, well-bound, with an indecipherable title on its spine. She almost always kept herself apart, reading or embroidering. She felt, and frequently failed to conceal, an overwhelming disgust at her mother's rather coarse and slovenly ways and her father's narrow-mindedness, particularly whenever the two of them quarrelled and when, as often happened, it was over nothing.

Signor Carlo told the maid to conduct Mabelli straight away into his room, and he retired into it to avoid the turmoil ('the revolution', he used to say) which the two ladies caused every morning when they came out of their rooms 'to tidy up the house'.

However, that morning Signora Erminia came out of her room with a skullcap on her head and a fan in her hand.

Marzani had made a present to them of a box at the *Argentina* theatre for that evening, and she was off to make some necessary purchases for herself and her daughter. The maid came on behalf of the daughter to remind her about a fan and some kind of greyish pearl ribbon.

'All right, all right... And what is she doing, the young mistress? Still in bed?'

'She is already up. She is combing her hair.'

'At eleven o'clock!'

Signora Erminia sighed and went out.

'Has Mama gone?' asked Giulia, poking her head out of the door of her bedroom.

'Just this moment, signorina. But don't worry, I have told her: the fan and the ribbon.'

'If she remembers!' sighed Giulia, going into the drawing-room. 'I'd like to know why she wanted to go out so early...'

'It is already eleven, signorina!'

'I know, thank you. She could easily have gone out with me after lunch today. It was she who said it was eleven, wasn't it?'

She stretched herself out on a rocking-chair, and began to push herself backwards and forwards, with her hands on the arms of the chair, her head bent, and the corners of her mouth turned down, as a mark of disdain.

'Well yes!' she added shortly after. 'We do have a lot to do in this house! What a bore! Olga, please fetch me the book from the table by my bed.'

She stopped rocking; she laid her head back, thrust her chest out and, raising her arms and locking her fingers, she placed her hands on her forehead, stretching herself out. Then she rose, and opened the piano, but she could not make up her mind whether or not to play.

The maid came back with the book.

'Put it on the table, there… I don't feel like reading any more.'

Once she was alone, she leant one elbow on the piano, making one or two keys shriek out, and she hid her eyes with her hand.

Under the pressure of her elbow, the keys kept up the sound for a long time.

For several days Giulia Antelmi had been aware of Lucio Mabelli's state of mind with regard to her. Those moments of reserve, those shy glances, certain cold words which fell from his lips, those hands which were always afraid of meeting hers, made it clear to her that he was already trying to distance himself from her little by little, while intending to remain near like a good friend, once he had made sure, without preaching and without making a scene, that she knew the reason.

But this behaviour irritated her. Already a strange obstinacy was starting to embitter her love. She was annoyed by her inability to conquer that man: she would have liked to compel him not to think so much, not to pay so much attention to the harsh necessities of his situation. And at the same time she was disturbed by every hint of recollection, which was blotted out immediately by a rush of blood to the head, and ashamed of the obstinacy which had obliged her to permit him, in order to bind him more closely to her and make it more difficult for him to find a way out, some caresses which were not entirely ir-reproachable. Lucio could not resist her, as he should have done, given his intentions; and this was in great part the reason for her shame; inasmuch as she allowed these caresses more because of a determination to conquer than out of love, and he went too far, more embarrassed than blinded, as if submitting to her in order not to offend her by holding back prudently.

Lucio Mabelli, when he came into the drawing-room, sur-prised her still in front of the piano, with her elbow on the keys and one hand over her eyes.

'Oh, Lucio!'

'Where is Signor Carlo?' asked Lucio hesitantly, and obviously put out.

'In the other room... Wait! Are you going off straight away?'

'I must tell him immediately...'

'What, immediately?'

'That he has obtained what he wanted,' he replied, showing all his zeal, as if to excuse himself. 'I'm sure he's expecting me: he said so to the maid... If I were to be seen here now...'

'In the first place, there's no harm in that! In the second place, Olga does not come in unless she is called. Mama is not at home.'

'Your father may come in here at any moment...'

'Well then, you will say to him what you have to say...'

'I would look so silly!' concluded Lucio.

She turned her back on him.

'That's all right... and you go then...' And she sat down with a sigh, that seemed like a yawn, on the rocking-chair.

Lucio simply could not leave like that. He went up to her, vanquished.

'You are unfair...'

'Unfair?' she asked, smiling. And she took the book from the table as if to start reading.

'Unfair, unfair... Don't you realise...'

'It may be so!' she sighed.

Lucio bent over the chair, to look at her.

'Am I leaving you in a sulk?'

Giulia raised her eyes from her book, and under his glance she smiled almost involuntarily.

'I am not, am I? Well, I'll go!' Lucio hastened to say.

But she held him by his arm.

'No. Why do you avoid every occasion for being alone for a little while and having a talk?'

'Me?'

'You, you; now, for instance…'

'But like this… If they saw us!'

'Don't you love me?' asked Giulia, lowering her eyes onto the book.

Lucio felt that this was the precise moment to explain himself to her. But how should he begin?

She hesitated briefly, and then she turned to look at him.

'What can I say to you?' he said, embarrassed and evading the question.

'Nothing?'

'One thing. It would hurt you too much, however. As it hurts me…'

'You love me?' she asked again, this time without hesitation, and looking him in the eyes.

'Yes, Giulia…'

'And this is how you tell me?…'

Then Lucio, urged on by her surprise and by his inner discomfort, and gradually coming to himself in his growing agitation, hastened to tell her – with some warmth, sometimes giving his voice inflections of impassioned sadness, and then exaggerating artistically, in that involuntary and unconscious moment – all that he had been brooding over for some time. He appealed now to her heart, now to her reason, blaming only the harshness of fate, the sad circumstances… He pointed out the false position in which he found himself in that house, and how much he suffered in being surrounded by the blind trust of her parents.

'And I am deceiving them, deceiving them…'

'Because you love me?' asked Giulia, trying to stem that flow of words by holding up against it from time to time, hastily, like a shield, some observation or question.

'Because I love you? No!' resumed Lucio, with his face

flaming red. 'Be reasonable! Because I cannot confess this love of ours to the one I should, and that's what's wrong. You should think of yourself...'

'Can't you? Why not?' objected Giulia once again.

'Oh, but you know why! You know what my position is... I cannot, and I think it is only honest to tell you, for my part...'

'Now you're telling me...' Giulia remarked; and into that *now* she poured all her scorn.

'Now...' stammered Lucio. 'But be fair! You knew...'

'You have said that you love me,' she replied, and her voice had become hard, almost resentful. 'You have taken my love... and how much of it! You have said that you love me!'

So then Lucio, almost weeping under the accusation, reminded her of that day when they went to San Paolo, and how they had found that they loved one another, without even suspecting it, as they were speaking of another love of hers. Did she remember? And he described to her his state of mind on that day. Who was being more thoughtful? He was! Certainly he would never have said anything to her. Her weakness was what had overcome him. Yes, yes. He no longer knew what he had said to her that day.

He loved her, and he had allowed himself to be drawn by his love, impelled by her... He too was young! Did not he too have the right to love, to enjoy life? But no, not at all! Youth claims its rights? Fate denies them. Youth complains? Fate laughs. To love? Work! And his work was without reward. And Fate, to be even more cruel, every time that she seemed to be less severe with him, caught him in a fresh snare! Ah, it was a great joke, a great joke!...

And he went on to tell her of all his dreams which had come to nothing, of his disillusionment, of his constant struggle to provide so many necessities, which disheartened him and distracted him from his ideals; and how difficult and laborious it was to keep himself faithful to that shadow of a dream, which was nevertheless the only reality in his life, his object and his *raison d'être* – Art!

In the effort to speak softly so as not to be heard in the other room, his voice had become harsh, almost hoarse, and at the same time he had a flood of words, and in them he breathed out all his real, intense anguish, practically weeping...

Giulia was moved: her resentment had gradually turned into distress. She took one of his hands and interrupted him:

'Don't speak to me like this!'

'It's true!' said Lucio indifferently, coming to himself again. 'I have never spoken of this to anyone. You forced me to.'

She had risen from her chair.

'And now?' she asked.

'You must think of yourself,' continued Lucio. 'Listen to me. I must not matter to you at all. I beg you: forget it. You have to forget.'

She remained for a moment with her head low and her eyes fixed, and let these words fall from her lips, shaking her head slightly, without moving her eyes:

'No... no... it's too late, at this stage.'

'Try...'

'Useless!'

She shook herself, gave a little shiver, she shrugged her shoulders, and she covered her face with her hands.

'What's wrong?' Lucio asked her gently.

'I don't know... I don't know...'

Lucio drew close to her, took her hands (she abandoned them to him without hesitation) and placed them on his breast, staring at her.

Giulia began to weep silently.

'I am fated...'

She raised her handkerchief to her eyes, and laid her head on his breast, and he began to stroke her hair lightly with his hand.

'Love me like this...' she said, in a voice that was broken by brief sobs. 'I am not asking for anything from you...'

And raising her head, with her eyes still swollen with weeping, and smiling a faint melancholy smile while her tears continued to fall, she asked him insistently, like a child:

'Will you?... Will you?...'

4

'We must speak about her...' Signor Carlo said quietly to Lucio, gesturing to the door through which his daughter had just gone out.

'About... the signorina?'

'I would like your advice, if you're able to give it me.'

'Advice?'

'It's a matter which is a little...' continued Signor Carlo, speaking in a low voice, and failing to find the right adjective. 'But with you at least I cannot have any secrets... Look, I'll explain. Do you know a certain... Arnoldi?'

'Antonio Arnoldi?' Lucio said immediately, going pale, and throwing his chest out, as though he felt a shiver in his spine.

'Precisely. You know him?'

'Why... are you asking me?'

'To have your advice...'

'I know him... that is... by name only... Excuse me, but why do you want to know?'

'I shall tell you...' said Signor Carlo. 'Yesterday I received a letter.'

'From Milan?'

'No, from Rome.'

'Ah, so he is in Rome then?' asked Lucio.

Why was he lying like this? He could not explain it himself.

69

Those words had come to his lips spontaneously, not looked for, not wished.

'It seems he has come here on purpose,' said Signor Carlo, with an expressive smile.

'Ah, yes! Of course!…' said Lucio; and then immediately he was astonished by this involuntary exclamation, which was in such obvious contrast to his smile, and which clashed with the ingenuous air which he had assumed to begin with.

But Signor Carlo did not notice any of that; he smiled with pleasure at Lucio's smile, and continued:

'In his letter he gives me the means of enquiring in Milan for any information which they can give me if I need it.'

'A proposal of marriage, then…' said Lucio, with his former ingenuous air.

'I thought you had understood that.'

'Oh yes, in fact…'

He was confused; he felt himself that he was confused. He wished to correct himself; and he made it worse.

'And he… what is he proposing? Him! Strange… I mean… well, he has been away from Rome… for some time, I think! And then, what qualifications has he got? What is he doing in Milan?'

And now Signor Carlo did notice his young friend's embarrassment, but thought that he himself had caused it by involving him in such a delicate matter. He took the letter from his pocket and offered it to Lucio.

'Here is the letter… read it.'

And they began to talk about the Ritter Bank of Milan, a German bank, very well-established. Signor Carlo had already asked for some information about it from one of his friends in Milan. Lucio too knew, from a friend who was employed in that bank, that it was very well-established. However, he could not understand how Arnoldi had managed to find himself such a good position – 'not for any other reason; but because the

Germans, you know, are so difficult... Secretary, dammit! a good post!'

'What do you think?' asked Signor Carlo, who was already laughing for joy.

Once again Lucio showed how embarrassed he was by the question. It looked as though it would be ages before he could leave.

'But... I don't know... you see... I could not say.'

'But,' Signor Carlo insisted, 'I don't believe, really, that it is a match that should be refused like this, without knowing...'

Lucio opened his arms in reply. Then he said:

'If you wish, I too can ask my friend for some information for you.'

Signor Carlo accepted, and was as usual profuse in his thanks.

Lucio left the Antelmi home a prey to unusual excitement, fumbling with a letter in his pocket – Arnoldi's letter to Signor Carlo. It had been left with him inadvertently! He realised that when he was on his way, and he felt that his hands were almost burnt by it...

It was already almost evening, and the Corso, with its lamps not yet lit, and quite in the dark, was crowded with people coming back from their afternoon stroll to Villa Borghese.

That great crowd bustling in the dark, pressed together by the narrowness of the pavement, continually having to watch out for the carriages which followed one another with such a great hubbub, made Lucio's head spin. He seemed to see Arnoldi in everyone; he felt that he would without a doubt see him there, suddenly, without a doubt.

And in fact he did see him. He was with some friends in the doorway of the Café Anglo-Americano opposite Piazzetta Sciarra, and he had moved behind the others politely, raising his arms as he laughed loudly, showing his white teeth under his curly whiskers, as black as ebony – a laugh that sounded like a horse neighing. Who knows why! Perhaps on account of some pleasantry uttered by one of his friends. His gold-rimmed spectacles had almost fallen off his nose. Lucio felt that noisy laugh grating on his nerves. Had he not laughed because of him, that idiot? He stopped all at once. He turned and stood still among the crowd to glance a moment in the direction of the café. He would have liked to go back and slap that dark insolent face… He started off again. To his home in via Laurina? No, not there! To Marzani's, then, in via dei Pontefici? And to do what at Marzani's? Oh, he felt the need to speak with someone, to pour out his heart to someone; and he felt that he was going there, to Marzani's, without really knowing why. But he had to do something! But what, and why? What was he complaining about? What was he hoping for? What right had he to obstruct that marriage? Obstruct it? Should he not rather consider it a stroke of luck, a liberation? Had he not felt irritation, scorn, anger after the scene which Signorina Giulia had made, weeping on his breast? Had he not called himself a fool a thousand times, and had he too not basely accused her, Giulia, maintaining that she wished to compel him, certainly not out of love, but out of spite or her yearning for a husband? Well then? There he was, the husband she wanted, Arnoldi! What was there left to complain about? 'Oh no! Not Arnoldi!' he thought as he walked along. 'Let the heavens fall, but not that!'

He found himself in via dei Pontefici, near Marzani's door. A doubt as to whether he would find him at home stopped him in front of the steps; but, without his realising it, he was halted also by the indecision which racked him and the need to get something clear in his mind before going in. He could not get anything clear at all; he pressed one hand against his eyes, and then, with a vague gesture as if to drive away all his worries, he started to climb up all the steps. As he went up, he felt himself shaken, relieved, by a mad impulse to laugh, and he crumpled Arnoldi's letter in his pocket.

Oh it was really comic, really comic the position he was in! 'Here I am! I must find a husband for the girl of my heart, and I want to find her a fine young man. Would they be kind enough to tell me about that Signor Arnoldi of theirs! Marzani? Poor chap… I do not say… he too could be a very good husband…' These last words were those of Giulia Antelmi. Lucio went over them in his mind, as he climbed the steps, still possessed by that urge to laugh bitterly.

He pulled the bell, and waited. Marzani was at home.

'Thank me! Congratulate me, my friend!' shouted Lucio, laughing like a madman in front of his friend, taking him by the arm and shaking him, pushing him backwards. 'You ought to congratulate me and thank me too, like Signor Carlo! Everyone should congratulate me! I am the most praiseworthy man in the world!'

'What's wrong with you? Let me go… Are you mad? What has happened to you?…' asked Tullo, gazing at Lucio in stupefaction, and attempting to free himself from his grasp.

'Nothing! What's wrong with me? I'm pleased with myself, can't you see? Was I not born only to be praised? Doing one good deed every day? It's no trouble, is it? And today I have done two, yes, one better than the other! And so there's a double reason for praise. Oh, that feeds my *amour-propre*! It'll grow fat on it, you'll see!'

'What have you done?' asked Marzani, stunned.

'What have I done? You will hear, my friend! Things that even the holy fathers tempted by devils in the desert did not do! Above all I have removed some fancies from the head of a girl of my acquaintance. The poor creature had had some illusions about me, just imagine it!… She has not thanked me, however: I expect to be thanked later! The poor thing thought I was a man like all the others, a man whom she might allow herself the luxury of fooling about with... That's enough of that! The other good action you know about. I have managed to obtain that post for dear Signor Antelmi. I have made him happy, so happy that he has immediately commissioned me to perform another good action. But first, notice, I wish to do one for you.'

'For me? Thank you!' said Tullo, who no longer knew whether to laugh or cry over his friend.

'No, you will thank me later,' continued Lucio, becoming serious all of a sudden. 'Listen, I'm not joking... Come here... sit down... read this letter...'

And he handed Arnoldi's letter to Marzani.

He immediately repented of it. All of a sudden – as if all those words which he had said with such extraordinary vivacity, in his growing excitement, had been reflected onto his suddenly awakened conscience – he felt a deep contempt for himself. He felt that his behaviour was unworthy; but he still did not see clearly the purpose of it, as if there were another person inside him, acting without revealing himself, for reasons that were still hidden from him. It seemed to him now that he had come to see Marzani as though dragged there by this other person, and he did not know why. Was it not useless, as well as unworthy? Signorina Giulia would never accept Marzani's hand, he knew. And yet, who knows? Tullo was rich, and not ugly, and he had never done nasty things like that Arnoldi. In an instant Lucio drew up a dispassionate comparison between the two, a physical and moral balance sheet... And now he would have liked to snatch the letter out of Tullo's hand; but he felt himself held back, as if someone inside him had said to him: 'Wait! What's done is done now... Let's see!'

Tullo read the letter, blushing at first, then gradually going paler and paler, until he looked at Lucio, bewildered, and let his arms fall to his side.

'So it's all over?'

'It's not all over at all!' said Lucio firmly, getting up from his chair. 'Signorina Antelmi as yet knows nothing of this letter.'

'Yes; but you told me...' stammered Tullo.

'I told you, if you remember, that Arnoldi no longer had any place in her heart. A girlish flirtation, I told you! Good God, you lose your head over nothing!... She knows now what sort of person Arnoldi is, and what he has done... It is not possible that she should accept him... And anyway, besides, I repeat that she still knows nothing of the proposal of marriage. You understand that Signor Carlo has given me, me... the job of asking for information on Arnoldi from Milan? Exactly! Well then, what do you want to do about it, you poor fellow? Trust me! Five or six days must now pass before the reply comes. Therefore you have all the time in the world to make your proposal to Signor Carlo.'

'And how can I, now...' observed Marzani, embarrassed.

'How? Oh God! Feign ignorance of it all! Because I do hope you won't go saying to Signor Carlo that I have been to tell you the great news! Besides, there would be nothing wrong in it... He knows that you love his daughter... and so... But there is no need to tell him... Go to him... make up your mind for once! And make your proposal formally. Believe me, the right choice between you and that man is not in doubt. Just imagine! They will welcome you with open arms!...'

Marzani smiled, still perplexed. He was glad to see, after what Lucio had said, that his task was a very easy one.

5

As Lucio had foreseen, Signor Carlo welcomed Marzani with open arms. Indeed the poor man had never expected such a stroke of luck. He had become accustomed to the idea of having to give his daughter away to an outsider who would take her far away, out of Rome. And he did not think that Marzani, good as he was, would do such a thing.

'He is too rich for us,' he thought. 'And my daughter has no dowry.'

Signora Erminia however had other ideas. For her Marzani was by now not only a fool, but someone who failed to keep his word. She was annoyed by the delusions and the hopes she had had of him which had come to nothing, and naturally she blamed him for this, rather than her own overheated imagination.

'It would be a very great honour for him to marry our daughter!' she said to her husband.

And Signor Carlo, so as not to incite his wife to further invective, opened his arms and submitted to the will of the Lord.

Both he and his wife now, seeing a desire realised of which they had no longer had any hopes, were so cheered up that for the moment they had forgotten the previous proposal and even Arnoldi's existence... Oh, and besides, a way out would soon be found for him! Meanwhile it was certain that their daughter, as the wife of Marzani, would remain in Rome, under their eyes. Faced with Marzani, Arnoldi had gone out of their minds completely. After all they did not even know him by sight, they did not know who he was... And so it had not even occurred to them that, in justice, faced with two proposals of marriage, they should not fail to take account of their daughter's choice. Signor Carlo, in his unexpected joy, had already practically given Marzani to understand that the marriage would take place; and the next day Signora Erminia spoke of it to her daughter.

From the beautiful bunch of flowers sent by Marzani the previous evening, for no particular reason, as a mysterious gift, and from the smile with which her father and mother had presented it to her, Giulia had suspected there was an understanding, and so in the morning she received her mother coldly. At her daughter's first words Signora Erminia felt all the expressions of jubilation which had risen from her heart forsake her lips.

Giulia was immovable in her refusal. Lounging on the rocking-chair with a book in her hand, she pretended to read, pushing herself lazily back and forth.

'A reason at least! At least give a reason!'

'I have told you: I don't want to.'

Signora Erminia finished up by losing her temper:

'What is your purpose? What is it you've got fixed in your head?'

'Nothing, nothing at all... Leave me alone, please. I shall think about it...'

'You will think about it, yes, but when? When you happen to have another opportunity, is that it?'

'I do not expect another...'

Yes, and so what a fine future she was undoubtedly preparing for herself!... She would finish up as a Sister of Charity, wouldn't she? Or a nun in some enclosed order! The usual story... Perhaps she was thinking like this because she still had her father and her mother, and a home... But she would not always have them, and then?... Oh yes, then what?...

'It's useless, Mama!' said Giulia, in order to cut short those rebukes. 'Now I have decided this: I will not marry! And you know, when once I have said something...'

It was in vain for Signora Erminia to face her with all the troubles suffered by girls who remain without a husband: enslavement to the ill will of others, solitude, discomfort, boredom... And what was the advantage in all this? She would certainly not be able to remain alone and apart: she lacked the means. But, even if she did have the means? A woman, alone, is never free.

She had immediately revolted against this scenario, with such liveliness and such efficacy that, for a moment, Signora Erminia felt as if she was under the spell of Lucio Mabelli's words, exactly as if he were speaking through her daughter's mouth.

Giulia did in fact every now and then repeat unconsciously some phrases of Lucio's, and she had more or less assimilated that particular way of speaking which was his.

'Well then? I ought to marry the first man I come across, eh? To avoid running up against all that you have described to me? So if I don't love this man, if I find him repugnant, it doesn't matter, is that right? Love? What is that? Does love come into it at all? And the heart? A mere nuisance! That's your reasoning! Those are your maxims! Hurrah for the people of good sense! And if I, in my inexperience, were to listen to you? Ah, you should have described this other scenario to me! What would become of me then? Answer me! What would become of me? How would I be able to live with someone who had inspired me with neither love nor sympathy, who, now that I was his wife, had not been able to make my girlish dreams come true?... Because that is how it is, and it's not my fault: we all have dreams when we are girls. My house would seem like a prison to me, my husband an enemy; I would fall into boredom or look for distractions. Oh, and then all the people of good sense, all those who utter prudent maxims as you do, would jump on me and accuse me of God knows what, and so on to the end! But what kind of wife do you think I would make – I, a girl whom you had forced to marry like this, without love? What do you want from her? What are your hopes of her? Ah, you can see, you can see that I know more about it than you do. I have my books, don't I? But these are the facts! I can speak of these things like this, between you and me; let it make up for all the times when I have to look as though I understand nothing... Go on, go on... And now leave me to read in peace, if that's possible...'

With her face on fire, and still quivering, she pushed back her hair from her forehead, and started to read once more, this time in order not to say anything more to her mother, who was still gazing at her in stupefaction.

When Lucio Mabelli returned to the Antelmi home with the reply from Milan he found a struggle going on there, an open war. Signor Carlo, in order to avoid seeing his daughter, shut himself up in his room when he returned from his work with Count Rivoli, and did not want to come out of it even to dine in company. He would have liked the earth to swallow him up, to avoid meeting Marzani again. Giulia too had retired into her room to avoid seeing the surly face and hearing the reproaches of her mother, who had thus remained as the sole mistress of the house. The one who had the worst of it was Olga, the maid, on whom Signora Erminia vented her anger and her ill-humour.

The reply from Milan had come to Lucio by return of post, one day after Giulia's refusal of Marzani's proposal. The reply recommended Arnoldi without reservation.

'And what's the use of this now?' Signora Erminia said to Lucio. 'My daughter wants to be a nun, you know. She has told me; she does not intend to get married, now or ever…'

'You have spoken to her also… about Arnoldi?' asked Lucio hesitantly.

'No, about Marzani, as you must know! But you must believe that, if I had spoken about Arnoldi…'

Lucio shrugged his shoulders without uttering a syllable, for fear that his voice might betray his inner agitation. Every word of Signora Erminia's seemed to him like a slap in the face. That irritating, coarse, vulgar voice got on his nerves. He felt that those fetters which he had dragged around for several months already with such sadness and such trouble were being riveted onto him again; and yet he still could not decide whether to speak or to put her off. On the one hand he was afraid to betray himself, and on the other he did not want to yield, to give in to that Arnoldi.

'Do you think that my daughter knows him?' insisted Signora Erminia.

'But... I really... don't know if I ought to interfere...' stammered Lucio.

'Please tell me... We think of you like a relative, just like a relative.'

'You are too kind... But look, it seems to me... that like this... without a definite reason, Arnoldi... yes... would never have done...'

'Precisely!' cried Signora Erminia, interrupting him, opening her eyes wide and slapping her leg sharply with her hand.

'At least,' continued Lucio, more quickly, 'he, Arnoldi, must have known the Signorina well, I think, or otherwise... You know nothing?'

'Nothing, nothing at all...'

'Well then, try that...'

The moment he had proffered these words, like a grievous and unwilling concession, Lucio felt a great weight had been lifted from his shoulders.

'Try?' said Signora Erminia. 'Today after yesterday's scene? Oh no, certainly not! She would be quite capable of saying no to me once again. You do not know my daughter...'

'But Arnoldi is still entitled to a reply...'

'That poor Signor Marzani!' sighed Signora Erminia.

At that moment Giulia came in, having heard Lucio's voice from her room.

'Excuse me a moment!' Signora Erminia said suddenly, seeing her daughter, and she added softly in Lucio's ear: 'I am going to tell my husband about it...'

Giulia smiled sadly, following her mother with her eyes.

Lucio too got up from his chair, embarrassed by this incivility in her presence. He would have liked to go away and never set foot in that house again. He had had to make an enormous effort to go there, after that scene in the evening with Marzani; and as he climbed the steps he felt it would be intolerable to have another dialogue with Giulia.

He indicated that he was going. She did not detain him; she sat on the sofa in her mother's place, and looked at him fixedly, with sorrowful eyes, saying nothing.

'I am going...' said Lucio, undecidedly.

'Wait, I wanted to see you!' she said, gesturing to him to sit down a little distance from her, and turned her face away.

Lucio sat down in the place indicated, and both of them, without looking at each other, remained for a while in a painful silence. Neither of them could decide to speak. Within himself he was angry at the sadness in her attitude and her silence: she was expecting laments and rebukes from him after the sad declarations he had made to her previously; and she, in her inertia and resignation, was inclined to accept them without making any excuses, being certain that he would not yield.

'You see?' he said at last.

She pretended not to understand.

'What?'

They fell silent once more, for a long while. Giulia was looking at him out of the corner of her eye, and saw that he was shaking his head slightly, with his eyes fixed, as if he wanted to say: 'He would not listen to me, and look what's happened...' And then she said:

'Because I don't want to make myself unhappy, hm?'

Lucio promptly turned to her, almost angrily:

'But who would want to make you unhappy?'

'They should all leave me in peace then,' she replied dully, her face changing, knitting her brows. 'I am all right as I am! You are all worked up about me... And what a scene! While I would be glad if no one in this house remembered my existence any more...'

After a brief silence Lucio pointed out to her coldly that she could not pretend that her parents were not thinking of her.

'Am I a burden to them?' said Giulia, and immediately she repented of going too far.

'It is not your present but your future that they worry about,' Lucio added coldly.

She was vexed by the somewhat ironical coldness and the air of indifference with which he was now speaking to her. Suddenly she livened up, and she too became sharp and superficial.

Oh, her future was all right! And there was time! And then, after all, it seemed to her that this future of hers should not only make others happy, but her too, just a little, shouldn't it? Just a little... Her ideas? Oh, yes! Well done! Her mother too had said that to her... Very odd! It must therefore be admitted freely that she was made differently from everyone else... They seemed to her so natural, 'her ideas', as he called them, copying her mother... And she began to laugh.

Lucio was left feeling awkward.

'Would you like to know one of "my ideas"?' Giulia went on. 'Do you feel cold in the winter?'

'Relatively...' he replied indifferently, as if going along with a child's whim.

'When you feel like that, do you think of putting on more clothes?'

'Certainly...'

'Now do you see? And that's what I think too! In summer do you leave some clothes off?'

'If you're making a joke of it...'

'Let's talk seriously!' resumed Giulia, raising her voice. 'Would you, Signor Mabelli, marry, for considerations which have nothing to do with love, someone for whom at the most, at the most, you feel only friendship?'

'Even if I wanted to, you know that I could not...'

Faced with that gaiety, which even in the midst of her lively gibes betrayed her affection, Lucio had completely lost heart.

'That has nothing to do with it! Oh God! I was speaking academically...' said Signorina Giulia, as though disgusted. 'Let us come to the concrete case, since you wish to. You have heard the great news? Marzani will have told you.'

'Your mother has told me...'

'That I have refused?'

Lucio nodded his head. Then he pointed out to her how she had displeased her father. Then he began to speak also about Marzani, and to sing his praises. It was clear that he was making himself foolish: he himself felt that, and he blushed because of it; but having gone that way he could not restrain himself any longer. Marzani had been a visitor at the house for some time; he was a good fellow; he had independent means; therefore he did not deserve that refusal...

Signorina Giulia gazed at him wide-eyed, in stupefaction.

'Why do you say this to me now?'

'Why shouldn't I say it?'

'You? It's ridiculous!'

Oh yes, it was ridiculous, really ridiculous, he had to agree, that he, he of all people, should come to speak in favour of Marzani, on an occasion like this!... Signorina Giulia could not believe it. Could her parents have charged him with doing this?

Lucio felt the full force of that terrible derision, and he smiled bitterly.

'Oh, it could...' he said. 'It's not like that! But it could even be...'

'Poor Lucio!' she exclaimed, commiserating with him with a touch of irony.

He was suffering terribly. He felt as though they had struck him with a whip across the face, and it seemed to him that, whatever he said or did, he would never get out of this imbroglio.

'You drew back, didn't you?'

'But because I had to!'

'And you yourself put another man in front of me, in your place: your good friend ...'

And Giulia had begun to laugh loudly. Ah, truly, history contained no record of a more amazing proof of friendship! Orestes and Pylades! It really was ridiculous...

Lucio rose from his chair resolutely; he went to her, and bending over her he said softly, but with a voice that trembled:

'I don't want, you understand, I don't want that, because of me...'

She did not let him finish:

'But it's nothing to do with you, my dear; put that right out of your head! Oh, you might like to believe that you are more precious than you really are? It's nothing to do with you! It's me, you understand? It's me who wants it like this. Is that enough for you?... It's not enough for you? Wait a moment...'

She rose, smiling at a whimsical notion which had come into her head; she went to the writing-desk and, taking a piece of notepaper from the drawer, she began to write, as a joke, a formal declaration: 'I, the undersigned, hereby declare...'

'How girlish!' said Lucio, gazing at her while she wrote.

'Imprudent, eh?' she answered, continuing to write with certain tiny movements of her head.

She folded the paper, and was about to entrust it to him when another idea came into her head. She reopened the drawer, took out a pair of scissors, and going to a mirror she took hold of a tiny lock of hair at the side.

'What are you doing?' cried Lucio.

'That's done,' she said, cutting the lock. She took a red ribbon from a casket, and knotted it about the hair, which she enclosed in the declaration, and thrusting it all into the inside pocket of Lucio's jacket, she said:

'Hold onto it! It will help you to salve your conscientious scruples…'

And she added, with a little grimace:

'Marzani does not suit me, and that's that!'

'And Arnoldi doesn't either?' The words came from Lucio inadvertently, unintentionally, in his confusion. And in his bewilderment he smiled, going quite cold.

'How does Arnoldi come into it now?' asked Giulia, surprised by the expression which had suddenly appeared on Lucio's face. 'Could it be that you are jealous?'

'They have not told you, but he is involved also,' he replied, with the same nervous smile on his lips, but with a different tone of voice, as though he himself would not say any more about it. And he stared at her.

'My little schoolfriend?' Giulia asked anew, more surprised by the way in which he was speaking to her than by what he was saying. 'How is he involved? Didn't he leave Rome?'

'It interests you? I will give you your declaration back…'

'How tiresome! Tell me how Arnoldi is involved!'

Lucio shrugged his shoulders as if he wanted to make her angry by exciting her curiosity.

'I don't know if I should tell you… He has written from Milan to your father. Or rather, not from Milan, from Rome. Because he's here, in Rome, come expressly for you… I have written to Milan… to ask for some information on him…'

'You?' said Giulia in bewilderment, hardly able to believe her ears. 'You?'

'I, I...' replied Lucio, accompanying the words with a nod of the head. 'At your father's request...'

'And why has my father said nothing to me?'

Lucio was at a loss.

'Almost at the same time Marzani asked for your hand.'

'Before or after?' said Giulia, struck by a sudden suspicion, which changed her expression and almost made her lose her composure. She did not give Lucio, who was staring at her in confusion, any chance to reply. 'After, certainly... Yes! Marzani must have known, without any doubt, of Arnoldi's proposal... Oh yes! he would not have made up his mind otherwise, poor fool!... It was you who told him? Tell me the truth! It was you who told him? It's quite useless to try to hide it from me any more... You? Oh...'

She put her face in her hands, indignant, shaking with shame.

'You did that? You did that?'

Crestfallen, Lucio made an attempt to justify himself:

'You know that... Arnoldi... is disagreeable to me in the extreme... However, mind you, I did say to your father that I didn't know him!'

'Go on... go on... I am grateful to you...'

'Marzani has always troubled me when he spoke to me about you... And so, yes, caught between two suitors, one in writing and the other in person, my position seemed to me so ridiculous that I could not resist the mad desire to tell him everything... Since I had to lose you, better...'

'Stop it! Stop it!' shouted Giulia, interrupting him, as though those words were choking her; and she put her face in her hands again. 'Shame on you! Shame on you!' she exclaimed.

Lucio could not think of anything else to say. It came to him in a flash that the hateful thoughts which could be glimpsed behind her words had truly been his thoughts – thoughts, however, which he had never admitted to himself, and which he was aware of now for the first time, now that his conscience was troubled. He could not object, it seemed to him right that he should be humbled, and resign himself to every affront. 'Provided that this is the end of it! Provided that this is the end of it!' he said to himself.

Giulia took her hands away from her face, which was fiery red, and without looking at him:

'My piece of paper! My lock of hair!' she said.

'What do you want to do with them?...'

She threw him a glance which was full of hatred and contempt; she tore the paper into a thousand pieces, undid the knot round the hair, and threw it all into the fireplace, accompanying the action with an exclamation of disdain.

Lucio made as if to go.

'Wait,' said Giulia. 'I shall call Mama.'

And, going to the door, she invited her father and mother to come into the drawing-room.

'Is it true that Signor Arnoldi has asked for my hand?' she asked them, the moment they came in.

And, without waiting for a reply, she added, 'You may tell him that I accept.'

Signor Carlo and Signora Erminia looked at their daughter in surprise, and then at Mabelli.

'Thank you, Signor Lucio!' exclaimed Signora Erminia radiantly, extending him her hand.

Giulia burst into laughter, and she ran towards her room.

A Friend to the Wives

It seemed to some of her friends, among whom was Paolo Baldía, that Signorina Pia Tolosani was somewhat affected by that vague melancholy which generally comes from too much reading, when someone has got into the habit of making the often blank pages of her own life conform to the model of those printed in some novels – but that without much detriment to her own spontaneity, thought Giorgio Dàula, another of her friends. Besides, that melancholy was very excusable, and could even seem more than sincere in a far-sighted young lady, already in her twenty-sixth year, who knew she had no dowry, and saw that her own parents were by now advanced in years. That was how she was excused by the lawyer, Filippo Venzi.

Not one of the young men who frequented the drawing-room of the Tolosani family had ever gone so far as to pay the slightest court to Pia, whether they were held back by the trustful friendship of her father and the taciturn kindness of her mother, or by the extreme respect which Pia imposed, obsessed by the task which she seemed to have set for herself of re-straining any action or word which had the least air of flirtation. And yet this reserve was adorned with the most graceful ease of manner, with the most exquisite courtesy allied with a certain air of benevolent familiarity, which immediately removed any newcomer's embarrassment; and yet they all saw in her the wise and intelligent little wife, and she herself appeared to put not only all her effort, but all herself indeed, into demonstrating that she would really be one, when someone eventually made the decision, without however being able to lay claim to any helping hand from her, or a glance, or a smile, or a word of anticipation.

Everyone admired the neatness of this house, which was cared for in every minute particular by her white hands; they all noted the simplicity and good taste which reigned there; but no one could make up his mind to court her, as they all felt that everything was going on very nicely there, like that, admiring and conversing amicably, without desiring anything more.

Pia Tolosani, moreover, showed no preference for anyone.

Each one thought, 'She would perhaps marry me, like any of the other *habitués*.' And if someone attempted to advance a little in her good graces, that was enough to make her distance herself with measured coldness, as if she had not wanted to give any scope for even the most harmless gossip.

And this was how Filippo Venzi, now married, had escaped her yoke which he had longed for, and before Venzi, two other secret aspirants. Then it was Paolo Baldía's turn.

'Then fall in love! You really are a fool!' was what had been said to him by Giorgio Dàula, his close friend and a long-standing friend of the Tolosani family.

'It's such a nuisance, my friend!' Baldía had answered, who was always bored. 'I've made two attempts with no luck.'

'Try a third time, for heaven's sake!'

'Who do you want me to fall in love with?'

'Oh for goodness' sake! Pia Tolosani.'

And so, in his compliance, Baldía had made a sort of start. Had Pia Tolosani noticed? Giorgio Dàula maintained that she had; indeed, he maintained that for no one else, not even for Venzi, had she betrayed her feelings as much as she did now for him.

'What do you mean, her feelings? She is impassive!' exclaimed Baldía.

'That's nothing! You will see. Besides, this impassivity is an assurance for you, if you are to marry her.'

'Excuse me, but why don't you marry her yourself?'

'Because I cannot, as you know! Oh, if I only could, as you can…'

2

All of a sudden Baldía had left Rome for his native parts. That disappearance had been commented on in all sorts of ways in the home of the Tolosani family. About a month later he returned.

'What's happening?' Dàula asked him, coming across him by chance, and finding him very busy.

'I have followed your prescription. I am getting married!'

'You're serious? Pia Tolosani?'

'Pia Tolosani indeed! A lady from down there, from my part of the world...'

'Oh you rogue! You were keeping her *in pectore*?'

'No, no,' replied Baldía, with a smile. 'It's a simple matter. My father makes a suggestion to me: "Is your heart free?" I answer: "It is free!" Well it was, more or less... That's it. I do not accept and I do not refuse; I say: "Let me see her; first of all, there must be nothing disagreeable about her". There wasn't? A good girl, a good dowry... in short I accepted, and here I am! Oh goodness, do I have to visit the Tolosanis this evening? Today is Thursday, unless I'm mistaken.'

'Certainly...' replied Dàula. 'Indeed, as a matter of propriety, you ought to announce...'

'Yes, yes... but I... I don't know, I find myself in a position... I have never said anything to Signorina Pia, you know; nothing has ever happened between her and me, and yet... You understand, I have the impression...'

'You must get over it! You would do worse not to go...'

'I would have an excuse: I have so much to do! I'm building my nest...'

'You are marrying soon?'

'Oh yes! These things should not go on too long... Soon, inside three months! I have a house already, in via Venti Settembre. You shall see it! Oh, but it's driving me out of my mind… Just imagine! setting it up exactly…'

'You're coming this evening?'

'I'll come, never fear.'

And that evening he did in fact go to the Tolosani home.

The drawing-room was more crowded than usual. It seemed to Baldía that all those people had come on purpose to embarrass him all the more. 'How,' he asked himself, 'does one go about announcing a marriage?' He could already have done so twice, in answer to questions put to him about his journey and his absence; but instead he had gone red and given vague replies. Eventually, when it was late, he made up his mind, seizing the opportunity provided by one of those present who protested he had so much to do at that time.

'I have more to do, my friend!' said Baldía.

'You?' said Signora Venzi, smiling. 'But you never do anything!'

'What do you mean, "never do anything"? I am setting up home, Signora Venzi.'

'You're taking a wife?'

'I am taking a wife… unfortunately!'

There was a general surprise. Baldía was snowed under with questions, and Giorgio Dàula tried to help him to reply to them all.

'You will introduce her to us, won't you?' Signorina Pia asked him at one point.

'Certainly!' Paolo hastened to reply. 'It will be a pleasure for me to do so!'

'Is she fair?'

'Dark.'

'Have you a portrait of her?'

'Not yet, signorina… I'm sorry.'

They talked about the house he had chosen, about the purchases he had made and those he had still to make, and Baldía in his embarrassment revealed how disheartened he was by the short time available and the difficulties in getting furnished. Then Signorina Pia, unprompted, offered to come with her mother and help him, especially in the choice of material for the upholstery.

'It's not your kind of thing. Let us do it. We shall do it with pleasure.'

And he accepted with thanks.

As soon as they had left the house, Dàula said to him:

'Now you are in good hands. You'll find yourself immediately relieved of all your problems. As with everything that Signorina Pia chooses, all your purchases will be good ones! She did the same thing for Filippo Venzi, and he is still singing her praises for it. She has the taste and tact that are needed, and also the experience, poor thing! This is already the third time that she has lent a hand... She thinks of others, since no one wants to think of her! What a beautiful nest she could build! Men are unfair, my friend. If I were in a position to take a wife, I certainly wouldn't have so far to go to find one...'

Baldía did not reply. He accompanied Dàula home, and then he strolled through the deserted streets of Rome late into the night, lost in a reverie.

She, she of all people, was going to help him set up house for another woman! And she had made the offer with the simplest and most natural air in the world... So then, had it meant nothing to her? that he... And he who had believed... who had blushed...

3

'Hurry up, come on, Mama! It's ten o'clock already,' said Pia, combing her hair through for the last time, and examining the result in the triple mirror on the chest of drawers.

'Gently, gently,' replied Signora Giovanna placidly. 'The shops won't disappear from the Corso! When is Baldía coming to fetch us?'

'Soon. He said about ten. That is, we said that to him.'

'But if you are suffering so much…'

'No, it has passed. Just my eyes; look: are they very red?'

'Rather red. They're also swollen.'

'It always affects me in this way, this headache! There it is, there's a ring at the door. It will be him!'

Instead it was Signora Anna Venzi with her inevitable two little children and the maid. These two pale and neglected little creatures were the source of constant distress to Pia. She had still not been able to induce their mother to dress these kiddies more cheerfully and boldly, and she was almost in despair because of it. Those long drawers, that sleek, straight hair, those little legs with their too-tight stockings really made her suffer. Anna, although she always followed Pia's advice slavishly, had, as a mother, remained coarse and stubborn. It was in vain that Pia had turned to her husband: Filippo closed his eyes or shrugged his shoulders in a melancholy way:

'Yes, I can see; but if her mother… I've other things to think about, signorina!'

Anna had come. She wanted to be there when they shopped for Baldía, urged by curiosity and not without some envy. The curiosity and the envy were perhaps mixed with a touch of still undefined jealousy, as if she had a presentiment that Pia would in the future have a closer understanding with the new bride than with her.

After so many years in Rome she had not managed to establish any friendship except this one with the Tolosani family, to whom she had been introduced by her husband a few days after her arrival in the capital. At that time Anna was very foolish, without any experience of life, and with no manners or charm. It was truly incomprehensible why Filippo Venzi, a cultivated and intelligent young man, one of the most outstanding barristers in Rome, had chosen her and taken her as his wife. She was not even beautiful, for heaven's sake! His friends had secretly admitted their disappointment, but no one had ever managed to guess, except perhaps Filippo himself, what Pia Tolosani must have felt seeing her. What! That woman? However, Pia had made her most welcome, and as time went on she became almost protective of her in relation to her husband; because Venzi, shortly after his marriage, had fallen into a deep melancholy, and truly none of his friends thought that this was without reason. Pia Tolosani began also to act as a mentor to Anna, and ultimately her company became absolutely indispensable to her. She chose the material for her clothes, she recommended the right dressmaker and milliner to her, she taught her to dress her hair in a less inelegant way, and to look after her home and enrich it gradually with all those trinkets which ladies know how to find in order to build a nest for themselves. She took the greatest care of all that. And she had even gone further.

Foolishly, Anna told her, time after time, all that happened between her and her husband, the slightest disagreements, the misunderstandings. And then Pia lent a hand to settle the first squabbles, very tactfully, without ever appearing, checking the anger of both of them separately, giving Anna wise pieces of advice and warnings of prudence, of patience…

'You do not know how to take your husband as he is! You ought to do this and that…' she said to her. 'You do not yet know him well enough. Oh yes, my dear! You see? In my opinion he needs this and that…'

To him, on the other hand, she spoke jokingly in a loud voice, preventing him from complaining and excusing himself:

'Quiet there! Venzi, you're wrong, admit that you're wrong!

Poor Anna! She is so good... You know, still rather inexperienced... And you, you strange fellow, take advantage of it! Yes, yes; but then, you horrible men are all the same!'

Anna now, after so many years of schooling and of residence in Rome, was, even by the admission of the disenchanted friends, much improved, it is true; but all the same she left not a little to be desired, especially by her husband.

'Not dressed yet?' she said to Pia as she came in.

'Ah, it's you, is it? Fine! Please sit down. Have you got the little ones with you? My goodness! How can we possibly take them with us?'

'No, they will stay here,' replied Anna. 'Tittí was screaming; I had to bring her with me. Aren't you dressed yet?'

'Don't you see that Mama can't make up her mind? Mama is moaning and groaning today. And I have a headache...'

'Let's put off the trip till tomorrow...' proposed Signora Giovanna.

'Oh goodness, Anna!' continued Pia, in order to change the subject suddenly. 'Pull that hair up a little! Up, up! How did you do your hair today?'

'Tittí was screaming...' repeated Anna. 'You fix it for me, please. When Tittí acts like that, I can't bear it, I can't.'

Signora Giovanna left the room, and Anna and Pia stayed to have a talk with each other.

'So Baldía is getting married, just like that, suddenly...' Anna began, looking at Pia as she dressed.

'Yes, indeed! It is strange: from time to time someone disappears, and then returns with a wife.'

'I don't know whether I should mention it,' continued Anna, 'but I could almost have sworn that Baldía was thinking of you; yes, so at least it seemed to me...'

'Not on your life!' exclaimed Pia forcibly, going red all over.

'I swear to you,' continued Anna in the same tone of voice,

'I thought so. In fact I said to myself: When will he decide? It doesn't matter at all to you, I know… But I…'

The maid came in to announce that Signor Baldía was waiting in the drawing-room.

'You go,' said Pia to Anna. 'We're almost ready now.'

4

Paolo Baldía was waiting for Pia in the drawing-room, in considerable anxiety. He was already annoyed with himself for having come rather too early. He wanted to discover, by paying closer attention to her words and her attitude, whether it was art or indifference which she had displayed the previous evening. But it could well be that very soon, once he saw Pia, he would be without the mental lucidity which that investigation demanded.

Between these four walls – where, until a little time ago, he had briefly cherished the notion of falling in love, where he might well have let slip some vaguely allusive words, or some rather expressive glance – he had a restless feeling of unease. Meanwhile he stood peering at the well-known objects hanging on the walls or artistically placed here and there. The image of his fiancée, completely different from Pia, was at that moment very far from his mind. Nevertheless he had quite firmly decided to love her sincerely, to treat her with the utmost care and kindness, to be for her at once a master and a husband: in short, she would be, after the great vacancy he had felt in himself up to then, the aim, the sole occupation of his life. But, for the moment, she was far away.

Anna Venzi brought her back to his mind, as she entered.

'I'm coming too, Baldía. I too want to do something for your… but look! You have not yet told us her name…'

'She is called Elena,' replied Baldía.

'She must be nice… I'm sure…'

'Quite…' said Paolo, shrugging his shoulders.

'You'll introduce her to me too, won't you?'

'Certainly, signora; with pleasure…'

At long last Pia came, dressed (it seemed to Paolo) with more care than usual.

'Forgive us, Baldía! We have made you wait a little… Now we can go! Mama is ready… That is… No, wait! Have you got the list with you?'

'Here it is, signorina.'

'Excellent! We can go. You've not bought anything yet, have you?'

'Nothing, nothing at all.'

'In that case it may not be possible to buy everything in just one day. Well, we shall see. Don't be in a hurry, and leave it all to us.'

On the way the interrogation over the fiancée began. Paolo, in order to strike an attitude, gave superficial answers, affecting indifference towards what he was about to do.

'But you are a strange fellow, you know!' exclaimed Pia at one point, becoming almost annoyed.

'Why, signorina?' responded Paolo, smiling. 'It is the simple truth: I still don't know her. You're smiling? I must have seen her, down there, give or take, twelve times. But enough of this! There will be time for us to get to know each other… I know that she is a good girl: that's enough for me, for now. You want to know her tastes; I don't know them…'

'And then if she is not happy with us?'

'Do not doubt it! Do as you wish; she will be happy.'

'Tell me the truth,' Pia went on, turning to Anna. 'Are you happy?'

'I, as you know, am very happy,' replied Anna.

'But your husband, at least, was not so disagreeable as Baldía; you will excuse my saying this, of course! What is the meaning of this air of indifference? You should be ashamed! Do you know that you will shortly be married?'

'Am I not mournful enough?' said Paolo jokingly.

'You should have seen Venzi when he was in your position! He was pitiful, poor fellow! Always obsessed by the thought that he might have forgotten something... And then, run here, go there; and we, Mama and I, behind: out of the house, to this and that shop... Ah, I assure you, no one could have done any more! But we were laughing... We did work.'

They went into a large soft furnisher's on the Corso Vittorio Emanuele. Two sales assistants immediately and very politely put themselves at their disposition. Anna Venzi looked in stupefaction at the ugly imitations of ancient tapestries hanging from the railings of the gallery which ran round above the large hall full of materials. Signora Giovanna looked closely at the displays suitably placed here and there and felt them. She did not wish to get involved in Baldía's purchases at all.

'What quality? You must tell me...' said Pia to Paolo.

'But I don't know... How should I know?' replied Paolo, shrugging his shoulders.

'Tell me at least more or less how much you want to spend...'

'Whatever you want to spend... I put myself in your hands completely. Act as if...' He stopped in time; he had been about to add: 'As if it were for yourself.'

'Mama, Anna!' Pia called out, so as not to betray the fact that she had understood why he paused. 'It's pointless talking to Baldía. Come on. For the bedroom a Byzantine fabric, right? Wide material... fine quality... Perhaps rather too dear?'

'Don't bother about the price!' said Paolo.

'You would save on the quantity: the Byzantine fabric is very wide.'

The business lasted a long time: they argued over the colour ('I adore the yellow!' protested Anna Venzi), over the quality, over the quantity, over the price… The young man who was serving them had very cleverly realised already! Oh yes! and he addressed himself to Pia alone:

'No, look, signorina; excuse me! Let the gentleman see…'

Paolo, who had been taken away from his books for more than a month now, and was being forced to regard as import-ant things which he would never be able to look at in that way, was already tired, and was looking out at the street, thinking. At one point, as he turned round, he saw the three ladies in the shop sharing a laugh secretly behind the back of the young man serving them, who had gone away to replace some material on the shelves. Anna particularly had her eyes full of tears, and all of a sudden she burst into laughter which she stifled in her handkerchief. When Paolo joined them Anna was about to tell him the reason for their laughter, when Pia held her back by one arm.

'No, Anna! I forbid you!'

'But what harm is there in it?' said Anna.

'None, I must admit!' replied Pia; and turning to Paolo: 'Do you want a laugh? Well, this is it. That fool has taken me for the bride!'

5

In his new house, which was more or less in order by now, Paolo Baldía was having a short rest, stretched out on the lounger in his study, where he was once again promising himself that he would soon begin a new life of thought and studying. He was expecting shortly the Tolosani family, and Filippo Venzi and his wife, who were coming to see his house. All at once it occurred to him to re-examine it carefully, one room after another, to guess the effect which it would make on his visitors. Another eight or ten days, and the nest would be ready to receive him with his bride.

As he looked at the curtains, the carpets, the furniture, he was glad to feel in himself a sense of care and ownership. And yet, during that examination of the house, one figure was constantly superimposed on that of his fiancée: Pia Tolosani. In almost every object he saw her advice, her taste, her foresight. She had recommended that disposition of the drawing-room furniture; she had suggested the purchase of this or that very useful and elegant object. She had put herself in the place of the distant bride, and had claimed for her all those comforts which a man, however much in love, would never have been able to think of. 'If I had not had you!...' said Paolo to himself. And he had himself bought some things in order to have Pia's approval, before that of his bride; knowing in fact beforehand that so many of those things would not be understood and perhaps never used by Elena, who was unacquainted with them and accustomed to living very simply. So he had bought them for Pia, as if it were for her that he had set up home...

At long last the visitors arrived. Filippo Venzi had as yet seen nothing, either of the house or of the purchases: Pia and Venzi's wife immediately took it upon themselves to make the appropriate explanations. Paolo took Signora Giovanna, who was a little tired, into the drawing-room, settled her down, and flung open the shutters of the wide balcony with the marble balustrade which looked out onto via Venti Settembre.

'Ah, it's delightful!' exclaimed Signora Giovanna. 'You go, Baldía. I'll have a little rest, and then I'll go round, taking my time.'

'Great progress!' said Pia, when she saw him. 'Almost everything's arranged already! Look, Venzi, look at those two consoles there, how nice they are! What they need is two nice vases of trailing plants! Does your fiancée like flowers, Baldía?'

'I think so...'

'Well then, two vases of flowers straight away!'

'I shall buy them, never fear. Well then, Venzi, what do you think of the house?'

'I like it very much!' replied Filippo. 'Very much!' he repeated, addressing Pia.

Anna looked at her husband, then at Baldía, and she abstained from repeating the same words.

From the dining-room they passed into the bedroom.

'I meant to mention it!' exclaimed Pia. 'We've forgotten them! Where is the holy-water stoup, the prie-dieu?'

'A prie-dieu too?' observed Venzi, with a smile.

'Definitely! Baldía's bride is very devout, isn't she, Baldía? Do you think that everyone is excommunicated like you?'

'And you pray in the evening before going to bed?' Venzi asked her wittily.

'If I had a prie-dieu, I would pray.'

Paolo and Venzi began to laugh. Paolo had never seen Pia Tolosani so lively, coquettish almost. Decidedly, she had either been completely unaware of that first very gentle attempt at falling in love, or else it had not mattered at all to her that he had discarded the idea. In either case, those outbursts of gaiety irritated him somewhat and almost attracted him. And while the memory of his fiancée faded and disappeared in her presence, she, on the other hand, seemed to be concerned only with his fiancée, spoke only of her, as if she wanted to protect her and keep her from oblivion; and she attributed to her, who was so distant, her own most exquisite thoughts, her own most delicate sentiments; so that Paolo was continually being made aware of her superiority in comparison with the other lady.

In stark contrast with Pia's gaiety was the ill-humour of

Filippo, at whom she was ceaselessly launching shafts of wit and joking reproofs. Her little voice seemed to be armed with needles, with some sharp stings amongst the sniggers. Venzi was smiling bitterly and responding with short, biting sentences.

For some time Paolo had been used to not seeing Filippo any more as the carefree friend he had once been; all the same, on that day, in the new house, happy now the work was completed, his friend's black mood weighed on him even more.

'What's wrong?' he asked him.

'Nothing, just thoughts!' replied Filippo, as usual.

'Venzi wants to change the world!' exclaimed Pia, teasing him.

'Yes, change it so that there are no women in it.'

'It won't happen! Tell him, Anna! What would you men do without us women? Tell him, Baldía!'

'Nothing! It's true, in my opinion. This house is the proof of it.'

Filippo shook his head, and went away to look over the house again by himself. Look, just look how Pia Tolosani would have arranged his house for him, if all those years ago he had been able to put a purse like Baldía's at the disposal of her good taste! How happy she must be to be able to give such a sample of her taste, her judgement, her foresight!…

In the dining-room he came across Signora Giovanna who was carefully observing everything minutely.

'Well arranged… one can only say… All in the best taste!' And to herself, thinking of her daughter, she was saying regretfully: 'How capable she is!…'

Anna, in that house, among Signora Giovanna, Venzi, and Baldía, seemed to be like a pedestal on which Pia Tolosani rose in great distinction.

'Now there's nothing lacking here but the bride!' said Pia. 'Sit down. Let's try the piano.'

And she played with deep feeling an exquisite composition by Grieg.

6

About three months after the wedding Paolo Baldía returned to Rome after a long trip, with his bride. Elena had been rather ill during the journey and, as soon as they reached Rome, she was forced to stay in bed for several days.

Pia Tolosani was dying with curiosity to meet her, and, from another point of view, so was Anna Venzi, who was anticipating the great pleasure she would have in demonstrating to the newcomer her own great experience and city ways (which she had learned from Pia). None of the friends had yet seen Elena; only Filippo Venzi had come across her fleetingly with Baldía.

'Ah, you've seen her?' Pia asked him, with scarcely repressed anxiety. 'Well then, well then, tell us…'

Venzi stared at her for a long time, without replying; then he gave his opinion:

'Um, curiosity killed the cat…'

'How tiresome!' exclaimed Pia, turning away.

'As I was saying, I have seen her,' Venzi went on. 'Signorina Pia, she was well, she was very well!'

'I am glad of it!' said Pia, rather annoyed.

'She was rather dejected, in fact.'

'Of course, poor thing!' exclaimed Pia, addressing Dàula. 'And tell us, Venzi, does his wife still have to stay in bed?'

'No, she is up.'

'Ah, we shall see her soon then!'

They had to wait a long time however. Baldía wanted to introduce his wife when she was well prepared to confront his friends and to satisfy their curiosity, especially Pia Tolosani's. But Elena, who was reserved by nature and rather stubborn, and tended to be short with people, did not allow herself to be affected at all by the way he saw things or thought about them. Nor was she willing to accede to her husband's wishes, although he always expressed them with the utmost politeness and tact. He could not even persuade her to wear the dress he preferred, or to take off from round her neck a certain ribbon which, in his opinion, did not suit her.

'I won't go otherwise,' Elena cut the discussion short.

Paolo closed his eyes and grunted. Be patient! He had unfortunately fallen in with a difficult character, who had to be taken as she was, firmly and tactfully at the same time; if not, civil war! But Paolo considered he was quite capable of doing this. His new wife was giving him plenty to do? All the better! A worthwhile occupation at last! And little by little, he had no doubt, he would mould her into the shape he wanted. Meanwhile, patience!

Emboldened by this feeling, he introduced Elena to Pia Tolosani, almost asking her in a veiled way, jokingly, without offending his wife's susceptibilities at all, for her wise and tactful cooperation.

When she saw Elena, Pia knew intuitively whom she had to deal with. She really did not like her appearance very much; but it was quite otherwise with her unbending and reserved behaviour, the unexpected glow in Elena's face when she began to express some contradictory notions, or the abrupt denials which she gave to her husband, who looked at her fearfully.

'No, no! impossible, impossible! He can do as he wishes.' That was Elena. 'He' was her husband; something, for Elena, very different from herself.

Pia looked at Baldía and smiled kindly. Paolo looked at his wife, and smiled in a rather embarrassed way.

'I like her; a strange little woman; I like her!' Pia Tolosani declared on Thursday evening to her friends.

Anna Venzi looked at Pia, rolled her eyes, and fidgeted restlessly on her chair.

'Ah, so she has come at last? So tell me, what is she like? What's she like? You like her, you say? You like her?'

Confidentially Pia admitted to Anna that as far as her appearance went, no, she hadn't liked her...

'Her dress was horrible... She doesn't know how to do her hair... Very ill-mannered too! especially with her husband... But almost, almost, look! I liked her like that! Baldía is rather conceited, don't you think?'

'Conceited, yes, I've always said that!' declared Anna.

At that meeting Filippo Venzi showed himself to be much more gloomy than usual.

7

Pia Tolosani's liking for Elena Baldía grew quickly, to the vexation and suffering of Anna Venzi. Elena, on the other hand, always wrapped up in herself, did not pay much attention to Pia; she accepted some advice from her, and from time to time she made some small sacrifice of her obstinate will to her, but only when it seemed to her that Pia's advice did not apparently agree with some wish revealed to her first by her husband. If he then showed himself to be too satisfied by the concession he had obtained, she withdrew it immediately, and Pia disliked that intensely.

'You see?' she said to Baldía. 'She spoils everything for me...'

'Have patience!' exclaimed Paolo once again, closing his eyes and grunting. And finally he would go out of the house for fear of losing his patience. Meanwhile, how kind that Pia Tolosani was! If only Elena had been able to feel some friendship for her! She would have opened up her heart and mind! The two women certainly would have understood each other better! And then Signorina Pia was so prudent, so judicious! She had such fine manners!… 'Little by little, who knows!' said Paolo to himself.

Where did he go? Accustomed as he was not to leave the house at certain hours of the day, he felt almost bewildered in the streets of Rome. He sauntered round a little; then, to relieve his boredom, he finished by going to Filippo Venzi's study. There, if nothing else, he would find something to read, while Filippo worked.

'Ah, it's you, is it? Fine! Find yourself a book and let me work,' Filippo said to him. And Paolo obeyed. From time to time he raised his eyes from the book and looked for a long while at his friend, who was intent on writing with his brows knitted and his head bent. How thin and grizzled his hair had become in such a short time! What an air of weariness on that broad bronzed face of his and in his eyes with deep circles round them! Filippo, as he wrote, bent his great head now to one side, now to the other on its Herculean shoulders. 'Unrecognisable!' Paolo said to himself. In addition, Venzi had lately become very caustic, even aggressive, and behind his sneering words was an inexplicable bitterness, an irascibility almost. Was it possible that it was the stupidity and vulgarity of his wife which had disheartened him so much and reduced him to this state? No, no; there must be some other underlying reason. What? Sometimes it had even seemed to Paolo that Filippo was cross with him… Why with me? What have I done to him? And yet, and yet…

One day Venzi began to speak to him of the Tolosani family, of the father, and the mother, and particularly of Pia, at first with subtle irony, and then with such a strange air of frank mockery that Paolo looked at him in stupefaction. How could he, their closest friend, speak of them like this? Paolo felt himself obliged to respond, to defend the friendly family, and he praised Pia, disgusted by the mockery.

'Yes, yes… wait, my friend! Wait!' Filippo said to him,

growing gloomy and yet continuing to laugh. 'Wait, and you will realise!'

A suspicion flashed across Paolo's mind; but he dismissed it immediately, blaming himself for being over-sensitive. This suspicion had however suddenly cast some light upon the change that had come over Filippo recently, and under this loathsome, persistent light Baldía rummaged about in his mind and gradually he saw his suspicion take shape as a monstrous reality. From day to day Filippo himself provided evidence that was more and more irrefutable. The last piece of evidence was the most distressing for Paolo: Venzi distanced himself from him; it got to the point where he pretended to be unaware of him so as not to have to greet him. By this time the only thing Paolo lacked was an overt admission, and he wished to obtain one, he wished at all costs to get a frank explanation from him. The idea came to him one afternoon when he was going home and he saw Venzi hurrying along via Venti Settembre. He went up to him resolutely and shook him by the arm.

'Will you just tell me what you have against me? What have I done to you?'

'You really want to know?' responded Filippo, turning pale.

'I really do, you know!' urged Paolo. 'I want a reason for your behaviour. I want to know because of our old friendship!'

'What a nice expression!' sneered Filippo. 'So you don't know? That means that the snake has not yet been cherished sufficiently in your bosom...'

'What snake do you mean?'

'You must know, that snake in the fable sheltered one snowy day by the pitying peasant...'

Paolo dragged Filippo by sheer force into his house. There, in the locked study, almost in the dark, he obtained the confession. At first Venzi refused, entrenching himself behind his usual almost savage backbiting.

'I am jealous of you!' he blurted out at last. 'Can you grasp that?'

'Of me?'

'Yes, yes. Haven't you fallen in love yet?'

'With whom? Are you mad?'

'With Pia Tolosani!'

'Are you mad?' repeated Paolo, in astonishment.

'Mad, yes mad! But understand me, have some sympathy for me, Paolo!' Filippo went on, in another tone of voice, almost weeping. And he spoke for a long time of his first love for Pia Tolosani, which had remained unknown, then of his marriage and the subsequent disappointment, of the void within him, of the terrible boredom troubled by a thousand irritations which had all gradually become definite and taken shape in the new despairing love for Pia Tolosani.

'Every day that goes by, my wife goes down, always further down in my estimation... She, on the contrary, always goes up! She is unblemished and untouchable! In our eyes, you see, she has remained as the ideal, whom you, stupidly, and I have let slip from our grasp! And that is exactly what she wants to show us, by having such care for our wives! And this is her revenge! Listen to me, and break away from her! Break away from her! Otherwise a year from now you too will fall in love with her, without fail... I can see it already... like me, look! like me...'

In his heart Paolo was sorry for his friend, but he could not think of a word to say to him. At that moment they heard in the corridor the voices of Elena and Pia Tolosani, who were returning from a walk together.

Filippo leapt to his feet.

'Let me go! So that I don't see her... so that I don't see her...'

Paolo went with him to the door, and when he was locked once more in his study, feeling very upset, he heard distinctly through the wall the voice of Pia, who in the next room was saying to his wife:

'No, no, my dear! Often you are quite in the wrong, you really must agree on that... You are a little too hard on him! And you shouldn't be like that...'

Biographical note

Luigi Pirandello was born in Sicily in 1867, and the island remained the inspiration for his work throughout his life (he even wrote, occasionally, in the Sicilian dialect).

In 1891, Pirandello took his doctoral degree in Italian philology from the University of Bonn. He then returned to Rome and began translating Goethe's *Roman Elegies* and writing short stories – including *Amori Senza Amore* [*Loveless Love*]. He became a professor of Italian literature in a teacher's college for women in 1898, and taught there for twenty-four years. In 1895, Pirandello had married Antonietta Portulano. Some years later she suffered a nervous breakdown, and Pirandello was forced to put her in an asylum. He, meanwhile, had begun to write plays, having hitherto considered drama inferior to the novel form. His work was ground-breaking, challenging conventional dramatic naturalism, and paving the way for playwrights such as Brecht and Beckett.

Between 1919 and 1922 Pirandello produced a large number of works for the theatre, the most famous of which is *Sei personaggi in cerca di autore* [*Six Characters in Search of an Author*] (1921). In 1923, he joined Mussolini's Fascist Party and, with their backing, founded the National Art Theatre of Rome. However in 1934 – the same year in which he was awarded the Nobel Prize for Literature for his 'bold and brilliant renovation of drama and the stage' – he fell foul of the authorities. His libretto for Gian Francesco Malipiero's opera *The Fable of the Changeling* drew adverse criticism, and the following year he angered Mussolini by refusing to support the Italian invasion of Ethiopia. Pirandello died not long afterwards, in Rome on 10 December 1936.

J.G. Nichols has published translations of the poems of Gozzano (for which he won the John Florio prize), D'Annunzio, Leopardi (a Poetry Book Society Recommendation), and Petrarch (for which he won the Monselice Prize).

He has also translated prose works by Foscolo, Boccaccio, von Eichendorff, Leopardi, Da Vinci, Petrarch, Casanova, Verga, Dante, D'Annunzio and Svevo, all published by Hesperus Press.

In 2004 a collection of his own poems, *The Paradise Construction Company*, was published by Herla Publishing (an imprint of Hesperus Press).

His translation of Dante's *Inferno* was published by Hesperus in 2005, and he is at present working on a translation of *Purgatorio*.

HESPERUS PRESS

Hesperus Press, as suggested by the Latin motto, is committed to bringing near what is far – far both in space and time. Works written by the greatest authors, and unjustly neglected or simply little known in the English-speaking world, are made accessible through new translations and a completely fresh editorial approach. Through these classic works, the reader is introduced to the greatest writers from all times and all cultures.

For more information on Hesperus Press, please visit our website:
www.hesperuspress.com

ET REMOTISSIMA PROPE

MODERN VOICES

SELECTED TITLES FROM HESPERUS PRESS

Author	Title	Foreword writer
Michail Bulgakov	*A Dog's Heart*	A.S. Byatt
Mikhail Bulgakov	*The Fatal Eggs*	Doris Lessing
F. Scott Fitzgerald	*The Popular Girl*	Helen Dunmore
F. Scott Fitzgerald	*The Rich Boy*	John Updike
Franz Kafka	*Metamorphosis*	Martin Jarvis
Franz Kafka	*The Trial*	Zadie Smith
Carlo Levi	*Words are Stones*	Anita Desai
André Malraux	*The Way of the Kings*	Rachael Seiffert
Katherine Mansfield	*In a German Pension*	Linda Grant
Katherine Mansfield	*Prelude*	William Boyd
Vladimir Mayakovsky	*My Discovery of America*	Colum McCann